Broken Noose

He was just another two-bit drifter riding out of the plains to try his luck in the town of Faithfull. But to Sheriff Horan, Judge Bream and a handful of others, he was the answer to a prayer – the man they would bring to trial, convict without question and hang for the brutal murder of the McCrindle family.

Simple, or so they thought, until Doc Sims and the bar girl, Cassie, chose to stand for the stranger's defence. Only then did the drifter, John Quarry, begin to reveal his hand, his quest and the dreadful retribution he would wreak on a town already lost in the making of its own hell.

Broken Noose

LUTHER CHANCE

A Black Horse Western

ROBERT HALE · LONDON

© Luther Chance 2005
First published in Great Britain 2005

ISBN 0 7090 7784 X

Robert Hale Limited
Clerkenwell House
Clerkenwell Green
London EC1R 0HT

Typeset by
Derek Doyle & Associates, Shaw Heath.
Printed and bound in Great Britain by
Antony Rowe Limited, Wiltshire

This is for RP

CHAPTER ONE

It was an hour after sun-up when the stranger rode into the dusty border town of Faithfull and Sheriff Horan knew he had his man.

He watched him for a full ten minutes from the shaded boardwalk fronting his office before summoning Deputy Frank Johnson to go wake Judge Bream from his usual whiskey-sodden slumber and tell him he was wanted urgently.

'And while you're at it, you'd better warn the others. A meeting, back room at Slaney's, in an hour.'

Johnson had grunted, settled his hat and narrowed a tight, piercing gaze on the stranger.

'You thinkin' what I'm thinkin'?' he muttered. 'He the man?'

'Best lookin' prospect we've had so far,' said Horan, lighting his first cheroot of the day. 'Drifter if ever I saw one. Wouldn't figure for him bein' missed.' He blew a curling wisp of smoke through clenched teeth. 'Get to it,' he added when the smoke had cleared.

The deputy slid quietly away in the direction of

Kelly's rooming-house. Horan waited a moment, his gaze still concentrated, the smoke still curling, then stepped from the boardwalk and followed the man at a respectful distance.

No call to hurry, he thought, no cause to spook the fellow. Let him ride easy, relaxed, just as he would expect at this hour in a quiet, uneventful town. He was making for Charlie Toon's livery, and rightly so. That roan mare he sat looked in need of rest. Been ridden all night, he wondered, taking the cheroot from his mouth? Could be. The fellow was carrying enough dust in his frayed coat and pants to make it seem like he had been hitting the trail hard and for some time.

A fellow on the run? Maybe not, figured Horan, replacing the cheroot between his teeth. He was too easy, too relaxed; there was no fidget, no backward glance. And no smell. You could always smell the fear of a wanted man. No, he would reckon this fellow for your average Plains drifter. Free-living, no commitments, no plans and no place to be save wherever he was. Faithfull would be just one more town to reach, pass through and never feel the need to see again.

The perfect drifter; could hardly have been better for what Horan and the others had in mind. Like the answer to a prayer, mused the sheriff, closing the distance as the stranger reached the livery.

And this fellow would be saying his last before sundown.

'Quarry . . .' pondered Horan, tapping a forefinger on his chin. 'Quarry . . . yeah, I heard tell of that name. You one of the Quarrys from out Montana Way?'

'Wyoming,' said the man without turning from tending his mount in the shadowy light of the stabling where a night lantern still glowed dimly.

'Wyoming, eh? Well, now, that's real interestin'. Ain't that so, Charlie?'

The livery owner grunted grudgingly and heaped another fork of muck to the growing pile.

'You got some problem with Wyoming, Sheriff?' asked the man.

'You could say that,' said Horan, folding his arms as he shouldered his weight to the wall. 'Yeah, I'd guess I do have some difficulty concernin' Wyoming.' His gaze darkened. 'There's a fella hails out of Wyoming I happen to be lookin' for.'

'Plenty of fellas raised in Wyoming,' answered the man, still tending his mount.

'Well, that's true enough, mister,' agreed Horan on a soft grin to himself. 'But, you see, I feel I kinda know this particular fella. I ain't got a name exactly, but I've sure as hell got one real good description. Like an eye-witness, you might say.'

Charlie Toon stopped forking muck and stared through the sun-dappled gloom.

The man turned slowly to face Horan, his eyes clear and bright, his gaze unblinking.

'That a fact – then you should have no trouble bringin' him in, should you.'

'You bet,' clipped the sheriff as he pushed himself from the wall and let his arms hang easy at his sides. 'So you just do as I say, Mr Quarry. Unbuckle that

9

gunbelt and don't go reachin' for that Winchester you've got sheathed there.' A Colt gleamed suddenly in Horan's hand. 'I'm takin' you in, mister.'

'On what charge?' asked the man.

'I'm takin' you in on the real gut feelin' I got that you're fittin' the description of the fella from Wyoming who shot Herb McCrindle and raped and murdered his wife, Louise, and daughter, Alice, at their homestead out at Panflats one mile from here on the night of June twenty-fourth, just two months back.' Horan's gaze darkened again. 'And if I'm right, mister, we hang 'em real high hereabouts on a charge like that.'

CHAPTER TWO

'Who is he?' Judge Bream wiped a shaky hand across his red-rimmed eyes, blinked, wheezed and dusted a smudge of day-old cigar ash from his moth-eaten waistcoat.

'Drifter, name of John Quarry,' said Horan, turning from the window in the back room of Slaney's saloon.

The judge sniffed and gazed quickly round him as if hunting down a hidden bottle of whiskey.

'How'd you know he's a drifter? He said as much?'

Horan laid an impatient hand on the baize-covered table and glared like a perching hawk.

'Not in so many words he ain't, but it don't take no assessin' from the look of him and them clothes he's wearin'.'

Storekeeper Marv Hinton cleared his throat importantly.

'He's a drifter, sure enough,' he pronounced with a lift of his head. 'I seen any amount. No mistakin' him.'

'Says he's out of Wyoming,' added the sheriff,

standing back from the table. 'Some ways from home, but that ain't of no account. Wyoming, Oregon, Utah . . . any place. What's the difference? It don't amount to none. Far as I'm concerned—'

'He know the charge?' wheezed the judge, his gaze still searching anxiously.

'Sheriff here's told him,' said Otis Slaney, smoothing the oiled neatness of his clipped moustache. 'Denies it, of course. Says he wasn't even in the territory two months back. That'll be his defence. But we'll say otherwise, won't we?'

'Ain't for bein' reminded,' sulked Harold Penney, the town barber, running his hands through the apron at his waist.

Slaney huffed and grinned wryly.

'Keen enough on the night, weren't you? Didn't see you backin' off none. There like the rest of us, to my recollection.'

'That's all very well,' began the barber again, only to be silenced by the sheriff.

'No call for goin' over what's plain fact and ain't for bein' changed,' he said, advancing to the table again. 'Truth of the matter right now is that the town's lookin' for a hangin' for the killin' of the McCrindles. And that's what we're goin' to have to give 'em. Soon.'

He paused, a finger tapping rhythmically on the table. 'It's either that or we – m'self, Judge Bream here; you, Slaney; yourself, Marv, and you, Harold, along of my deputy – wait on the day when somebody here is goin' to get to askin' some mighty awkward questions about that night out on the Pan. And mebbe, just mebbe, come up with some troublin' answers concernin' ourselves.'

He gazed carefully round the faces watching him. 'So the man from Wyoming – an out-and-out, two-bits drifter, of no reckonin' if ever I clapped eyes on one, and currently locked secure in the town jail – ain't for bein' taken lightly. Like I figured soon as I saw him, John Quarry is the answer to our prayers.'

The storekeeper stiffened his shoulders.

'The sheriff's right. The town's angry, ready to flare. There's a nasty smell about.' He sniffed loudly. 'I ain't slept decent since that night, and I ain't for makin' no bones about it, so there's got to be a way out. If this fella, Quarry, is that way, we take it, no messin'.' He sniffed again. 'What do you reckon, Judge?'

Judge Bream wiped a hand over his sweat-beaded face. 'I need a drink,' he croaked.

Slaney stepped to a cupboard, opened the door, produced an unopened bottle of whiskey and a glass and placed them on the table.

'Help yourself,' he grinned. 'It's on the house.'

Harold Penney fidgeted uncomfortably while the judge poured a generous measure and sank it in one noisy gulp.

'T'ain't goin' to be as easy as that,' stuttered the barber, beginning to twitch. 'Fella's mebbe goin' to call for some advocate to stand to him. He'll mebbe want to question witnesses, see the evidence. Hell, he ain't goin' to take it sittin' down, is he.'

'You can leave that to me,' said the judge, refilling his glass. 'If he's our man – and he's all we've got right

13

now – so be it, he'll hang by the power of attorney vested in me.' He gulped another measure, then belched. 'Any chance of a decent breakfast round here? Steak'll do fine. Keep it a mite rare.'

'I'll see to it,' said Slaney. 'Meantime, I suggest we don't waste any time over this matter. We get movin', eh, Sheriff? No reason why we shouldn't set the trial for today, is there?'

'None as I can see,' agreed Horan. 'Early tonight, here in the saloon. That soon enough?'

'Perfect,' smiled the storekeeper. 'Trial tonight, hangin' at sun-up. And that'll be an end of it.'

Slaney produced more glasses and poured a measure in each.

'We'll drink to that.'

Doc Sims waited in the shade of the boardwalk some distance from Slaney's saloon, his gaze tight on the batwings, his fingers flexing at his sides. Things were looking bad, he mused, and likely to get a whole sight worse if even half of his suspicions were confirmed.

Situation was already clear enough: a man, a stranger, said to be from Wyoming, had ridden into town soon after sun-up and promptly been arrested and jailed by Sheriff Horan on a charge of murder and rape. The man responsible for the massacre and bloodbath out at the McCrindle spread had been brought to book – or so the folk of Faithfull now believed.

There would be a trial, Judge Bream presiding, and the verdict never in doubt: the stranger would be pronounced guilty and would hang before noon tomorrow, if Doc Sims knew Horan, and that would be that. The town would be satisfied and go back to being quiet, dusty, a nowhere place on the border where the stage stopped once in every two months and no one stayed to visit.

No one, that is, save dirt-trail drifters who wandered in from the Panflats.

Doc's gaze narrowed as the batwings swung open and the sheriff, Marv Hinton and Harold Penney stepped to the boardwalk, paused in animated conversation and continued for a full three minutes before going their separate ways.

Doc waited in the shade, his eyes concentrated now on the town barber as he made his nervy way back to his shop, unlocked the door, ran up the shutters and prepared for business.

Doc would be his first customer this morning. But not for a shave.

'Mornin', Doc. Say, you're about early,' beamed Penney. 'Lookin' to a shave? I got one of them new afters, real pleasant. Came in on the stage last time round. Just a few cents a splash. Care to sample?'

'I ain't here for no afters, Harold, or for a shave come to that. I'm here because of what's been happenin' in this town since sun-up. And don't say you haven't heard or ain't a party to whatever Sheriff Horan's plannin'.'

The barber shuffled uncomfortably, looked away, then at the array of combs and scissors on the side table.

'Only doin' his duty, I guess,' he muttered, fingering the tools of his trade. 'He is the law hereabouts.'

'Law's one thing, trumpin' up a charge against a fella who just happens to have drifted into town – and likely as not innocent enough – is somethin' else.' Doc adjusted the set of his frock-coat. 'What's Horan got in mind? A trial, soon as he can fix it and sober up Judge Bream? That it?'

'Somethin' like,' said Penney, still fingering a comb. 'Goddamnit, Doc, we can't stand back and let the McCrindles die for nothin'.' He turned from the table and stared directly into the doc's eyes. 'Town wants a hangin'. You know that. We all know it. And that's what it's goin' to get.'

'We'll see,' grunted Doc Sims as he strode back to the sunlit street and headed for the mercantile.

CHAPTER THREE

'I'm a busy man, Doc. Got a business to run here. Don't run itself, you know.' Marv Hinton emerged from behind stacked barrels of molasses and sacks of flour, his hands turning like bagged birds in the folds of his black apron. 'What's the problem?'

Doc Sims gazed slowly round the stocked and neatly arranged store, the packed shelves, piled blankets, tools, handles, tins and pails, hanging clothes and polished counter.

'Say one thing for you, Marv, you always keep a tidy ship. Neat as a pin, clean as a whistle. A credit to you.'

'Nice of you to say so, but it don't just happen. Calls for hard work and dedication.'

Doc smiled quietly to himself. 'I'm sure,' he murmured. 'A lifetime's work when you come to reckon it.'

'Very true,' agreed Hinton, his impatience beginning to show. 'Look, I ain't for hurryin' you, Doc, but there's things—'

'You've already had a busy start to your day.'

Hinton's gaze tightened. His hands were suddenly still.

'What's that supposed to mean?'

'I think you know what I'm talkin' about, Marv,' said the doc in a carefully measured tone, his own gaze equally tight and steady. 'The stranger who hit town first light, who's now sittin' it out in the jail back there – doubtless wonderin' what in the name of hell's teeth has hit him.'

'John Quarry,' clipped the storekeeper, now releasing his hands from the black apron. 'A drifter out of Wyoming, no mistakin' that. Charlie Toon'll tell you the same. That horse he rode in ain't seen stablin' in months.'

'It ain't his horse I'm botherin' to, or where he hails from; it's what he's sittin' in that jail charged with and just what precisely is goin' to happen to him that concerns me.'

The storekeeper's hands went back to the apron as he moved past Doc Sims to the open doorway.

'Horan's certain the fella was out at the McCrindle spread on that night. Judge Bream agrees – and so, as a matter of fact, do I. Fella'll stand trial tonight. We've had a meetin'. It's been agreed.'

'Oh, sure, it's been agreed,' flared the doc, the colour rising to his cheeks. 'I'll bet it has – by the handful of folk with the most to lose!'

Hinton spun round, his eyes gleaming.

'What you sayin' there, Doc?'

'I'm sayin' what I've always said ever since I was called to examine the bodies you and the others say you found that night: that what happened to McCrindle, his wife and daughter was not the work of one man. There were others involved, mebbe up to

18

half a dozen men. That was gang rape and murder, and there ain't no disputin' it. And I might have proved it, if you and Horan, the judge and others hadn't been so darned anxious to bury the bodies.' He paused a moment, his stare icy. 'As for the fella sittin' there in jail—'

'If you've got any more to say on the matter, I suggest you address yourself to Sheriff Horan and Judge Bream.'

'You goin' along with this so-called trial, Marv? You goin' to stand by and let it happen?'

The storekeeper stiffened. 'I've told all I know about the McCrindle killin'. There ain't nothin' more to be said except to find and bring to trial the man who did it.'

'They'll hang him,' said the doc, his gaze darkening. 'You know that, don't you, Marv? They'll hang him high. And that'll be another murder.'

Judge Bream finished his plate of prime steak, dabbed the napkin at his lips, poured himself another whiskey and slumped back in the chair, his watery, bloodshot eyes settling wearily on Sheriff Horan's face.

'So what's the problem now?' he asked, making no attempt to stifle the belch that rocked his ample paunch.

'Doc Sims,' said Horan bluntly, continuing to pace the length of Slaney's shadowy saloon bar. 'He's back on his old hobby-horse: questionin' the McCrindle killin', tellin' Marv again as how he could have proved that more than one man was involved.'

'And doubtless he could,' grunted the judge, resting his hands on his paunch. 'Wouldn't have been difficult – and he *knows* it wouldn't. Damnit, he's a physician, he knows about these things, knows what to look for. But he didn't get the chance, did he? We made certain of that. Leastways, you did.'

The sheriff turned at the end of the bar, and measured his steps to the batwings.

'Says I've got no right to jail the drifter, much less put him on trial. Says there ain't a stitch of evidence to support the charge.'

'And he's right again, ain't he,' said Bream, beginning to pick at the frayed edges of his waistcoat. ' 'Course he is. Doc Sims is nobody's fool. He's mebbe already figured what really happened that night. That wouldn't take no genius to work out. But the point is, he ain't got no proof, knows full well there weren't no witnesses, and reckons, quite rightly, that one man's theorizin' ain't goin' nowhere while I'm presidin' hereabouts.' He finished the whiskey and belched again. 'So what you worryin' about?'

Horan lit a cheroot and blew a thin line of smoke to the street.

'He's like an irritatin' burr in my boot,' he mouthed sullenly.

Judge Bream poured himself another generous measure of whiskey.

'Well, mebbe you should change your socks, eh?'

Otis Slaney watched the woman settle the pleats and folds of her dress, tease her hair into neat waves and curls again, and smiled softly.

'You're still a good-lookin' gal, Cassie,' he said, propping himself comfortably at the side of the window overlooking the street. 'Still one of the best, eh?'

'And no thanks to you, Otis Slaney,' she huffed, with a toss of her head and swish of the dress. 'No thanks to this two-bits town neither. Time I moved on.'

'You've been sayin' that for the past five years to my certain knowledge,' grinned the saloon owner. 'You're still here.'

'Yeah, well, that's a force of circumstance, ain't it. Lack of funds, as they say. If you paid me a decent—'

'Sure, sure, I've heard it all before, but the fact of it is, my dear, you know well enough which side of the corral has the shade, don't you. Roof over your head, clothes, food, safety – and all I ask is that you run your side of the business efficiently and profitably. 'T'ain't askin' a lot.'

The woman crossed to Slaney's side at the window and stared into the street. 'What about that man the sheriff's holdin'?' she asked quietly.

'What about him?'

'You goin' along with this trial I hear they're stagin'?'

'Of course,' said Slaney. 'And why not? Time somebody came to book for the McCrindle killin'.'

'Sure, but not some innocent drifter who just happened along of this dump. That ain't no justice.' Cassie flashed a piercing glance at Slaney. 'That'll be murder if you get to hangin' him.'

'He'll stand to a fair trial,' said Slaney, pushing himself from the wall. 'Judge Bream'll see to that.'

'Some trial! Some justice with that drunken sonofabitch presidin'!' Cassie ran her hands down her hips. 'You know as well as I do the whole darned thing will be fixed tighter than my stays. The fella will hang and that'll be that. Murder. And the real scum responsible will go on breathin'.'

Slaney fingered his oiled moustache, smiled briefly before clamping a tightening grip on the woman's arm.

'Stay out of things that don't concern you, Cassie. And keep them tasty lips of yours buttoned. Like I said, you've got the shady side of the corral right now. Keep it that way. The other side's sheer hell.'

CHAPTER FOUR

The town gathered early that night, leaving their homes, the scattering of outlying spreads, the few rough shacks, to assemble in the shadows at Slaney's saloon soon after sundown.

At first they stood about in quiet groups, some happy enough to listen to the latest gossip concerning the drifter from Wyoming, others to speculate on who he might really be, how long he had been in the territory, where he could have been heading, but more alarmingly why he had stayed so close to the scene of the grisly crime.

'I heard say as how it's all part of the madness,' said a tall, rangy man. 'Kinda reliving it all again. Weird.'

'Mebbe he's full of remorse,' opined a fellow in spectacles. 'Mebbe he's seekin' salvation.'

'Yeah,' leered a man between spits, 'and he'll sure as hell get some here – swingin' at the end of a rope if I have my way.'

Mention of a hanging raised a chorus of approval.

'Tell you somethin', folks,' said a thickset man with a bullock chest, 'Herb McCrindle will rest a whole lot easier when it's done. You can bet to that.'

'And his woman,' piped a supporter through a drift of pipe smoke. 'Weren't no rhyme or sense to killin's like that. I ain't heard of none worse, not nowhere.'

The bullock-chested man had stepped to the boardwalk.

'Well, let's just make sure there's no likelihood of such bein' heard of never again. It's time for retribution. Let the town of Faithfull show the way to justice. . . .'

The call had been greeted by cheers and a lifting of spirits – among some, but not all. Marv Hinton for one; he was sweating. Harold Penney for another; he had closed down early, opened a bottle of quality whiskey and sunk three stiff measures before venturing towards Slaney's. Now he too was sweating, but he reckoned that was due to the sticky night air and not his fear of the prospect ahead. Damn it, it would all be over in a couple of hours. Cut and dried. No problem. Just like Horan and Judge Bream had said. There were some things in life that were certainties.

The outcome of this night's doing would be one of them.

Cassie had ushered her four bar girls into the saloon's deepest shadows long before the townfolk began to fill the bar and take their seats. She had placed them under strict orders.

'No mixin' it tonight, girls. No trade and no drinkin',' she had told them firmly. 'There's goin' to be some high spirits hereabouts in a couple of hours, and

I ain't for havin' you bein' a part of it. You stay put.'

She had then joined Doc Sims where he stood at the far end of the already smoke-hazed bar in what little there was of a fresher air through the batwings.

'A bad business, Cassie,' he murmured, making room for her at his side. 'This ain't no way to run a town.'

'Any way it can be stopped?' She frowned, watching the crowd assemble.

'Would you like to try, knowin' the mood these folk are in? There ain't a man standin' who'd risk that right now.'

Cassie nodded nervously, patted her hair and smoothed her dress.

'He'll hang,' she muttered flatly.

'You can bet to that,' grunted the doc.

The bullock-chested man pushed through the 'wings and watched the scene with a look of satisfaction on his sweat-streaked face.

'The night of reckonin', eh, Doc?' He grinned. 'Now we get to hear what really happened out at McCrindle's.'

'You don't expect that fella back there is goin' to tell you, do you?' said Sims.

'Don't see why not. What's he got to lose, anyhow? Might as well come clean. He ain't goin' no place.'

'Suppose he didn't do it,' said Cassie. 'Suppose he ain't the man.'

'No supposin' about it to my figurin', Miss Cassie,' smiled the man. 'He was out there at the spread, you can bet to that. Sheriff Horan ain't nobody's dumb mule.'

Doc Sims bit back on voicing his further thoughts, his quick glance urging Cassie to do the same.

'You'll get nowhere arguin' with a fella like that,' he said when the man had moved on. 'His mind's made up, same as it is with most here.'

'That's dangerous,' hissed Cassie, her eyes darkening.

'You don't have to tell me, my dear.'

Marv Hinton called above the babble of voices for quiet.

'Time we got started,' he announced, adjusting the set of his coat, smoothing the collar. 'Seems like we're all here, so there ain't no point in delayin'.'

'Too right there ain't!' quipped bullock-chest to a general murmur of approval.

'Quite so,' coughed the storekeeper, adjusting his coat again. 'First things first. Judge Bream here wishes to address you.'

The gathering's attention turned to the judge seated at the table that had been set aside at the head of the bar. A lantern flickered dimly to his left, a bottle and glass gleamed alongside his gavel to his right. Smoke drifted from the cigar between his fingers, the ash thickening menacingly. His jacket was as moth-eaten as his waistcoat, the derby set slightly askew on his head, as worn and frayed as the rest of his attire.

He blinked his still bloodshot eyes and began.

'Let's get one thing straight: this is my court under my jurisdiction. I ain't for hearin' no opinions from the floor. Anybody got anythin' to say – anythin' worthwhile, that is – will rise to ask for time to speak.

I'll decide if he gets it. No messin'. Anybody inter-ruptin', causin' a fracas – that's trouble to you – will be thrown out on his ear and mebbe face a charge of contempt come sun-up. That clear enough?'

'You got it, Judge,' said a man in the shadows.

'Good.' The bloodshot gaze tightened. 'By the powers vested in me, and true to my honourable callin', I run a fair court, but there'll be no shenani-gans, no mob behaviour. Law and order is the demand. See that I get it, every last one of you.'

'He's sober for once,' whispered Cassie.

'But for how long?' murmured Sims.

The judge drew heavily on the cigar, wheezed as he released a long trail of smoke to the ceiling, tossed the butt to a spittoon where it hissed loudly, and banged his gavel on the table.

'I declare this court in the town of Faithfull, County of Marianne, in session, Judge Theodore Bream presidin'. Bring out the prisoner.'

The door to Otis Slaney's office and private quarters was opened carefully, then with a confident flourish as Sheriff Horan and deputy Frank Johnson escorted John Quarry to a table in the smoke-hazed glow of a polished lantern. They prodded the prisoner to stiffen his shoulders and steady his gaze. The man merely grunted and obliged.

'Calm enough, ain't he,' said Cassie softly. 'He ain't even broken sweat.'

Nor had he, thought Doc Sims, his gaze concen-trating on the accused drifter. The pale-blue eyes in a scrawled, weathered face were calm, the stare ahead steady and untroubled as if the thoughts behind them were some place else, distant and unknown. But John Quarry was missing nothing. Sims had noted quick enough the soft, irregular twitch of a nerve in the man's left cheek, a movement that came and went on the lift and tone of the voices around him.

It twitched again as Judge Bream cleared his throat, wiped his eyes and began to speak in a gravelled, smoky voice.

'Your name John Quarry?'

'It is,' answered the man.

'You out of Wyoming?'

'Some long time back, yes.'

'I ain't interested in the chronological detail. Just answer the question: yes or no.'

'Yes.'

'You heard the charge brought against you by Sheriff Horan?'

'I've heard it.'

'And how are you pleadin': guilty or not guilty?'

'Not guilty,' said the man firmly.

There was a buzz of murmuring among the gathering.

Judge Bream's gavel brought the bar to order.

'You speakin' for yourself in your defence?'

'No, he ain't,' called a voice from the batwings. Doc Sims threaded his way through the array of tables, bodies, staring eyes and amazed expressions.

'I am,' he announced defiantly.

CHAPTER FIVE

'Just what in hell is goin' on? Will somebody tell me, f'cris'sake?' Marv Hinton pulled irritably at his coat, the laced tie at his collar, drew a large bandanna from his pocket and mopped his face. 'Well?' he croaked. 'Lost your voices?' He turned back to the window in Slaney's office and stared wide-eyed into the night. 'This all goin' to go wrong?' he murmured, as if addressing a hidden body.

'No problem,' said Judge Bream, pouring himself another measure of whiskey at the baize table. 'Fella's got himself a counsel, somebody to speak on his account. Doc Sims – misguided as he might be – has asked for an adjournment to prepare a defence. I've granted him 'til noon tomorrow. All legal and above board. Can't argue with that. Noon tomorrow, not two shakes of a gnat's leg longer.'

'But Doc, for heaven's sake. Who'd have thought it?' Harold Penney licked a forefinger and plastered a stray hair into place.

Otis Slaney blew cigar smoke and wafted it clear of his moustache.

'Who indeed,' he muttered, one eye on the judge's growing consumption of the bottle of best whiskey.

'I would,' said Horan from where he stood at the door. 'Doc Sims ain't never been satisfied with what he found that night. Said as much, and more than once. And he still ain't settled none. Still gnawin' at it like a rat at a barley barrel. He sees doin' what he's doin' as openin' up the whole darned issue yet again. And I for one don't like it.'

'Me neither,' agreed Slaney. 'We're movin' into dangerous waters.'

'Never mind what we're movin' into, that's bad enough,' croaked Hinton, turning again at the window. 'You seen the mood of the town? You heard them? They ain't one bit happy. Damn it, they were expectin' a hangin' come sun-up.'

'Well, they're goin' to have to wait, aren't they,' wheezed the judge, finishing another measure. 'There's a procedure here, and we're goin' to have to go along with it if the outcome, the final verdict, is goin' to look anythin' like legal.' He blinked and stared at the bottle in front of him. 'They'll get their hangin'. You've got my word on it.'

Hinton pulled at his coat again and relaxed.

'That much at least is reassurin'. And that said, I propose we leave the legalities to Judge Bream and meantime turn our attention to the townfolk. It's them we've got to watch.'

'Leave them to me,' said Horan. 'They won't be no trouble. It's Doc who worries me.'

'That burr in the boot again, eh, Sheriff?' The judge smiled, reaching for the bottle again. 'Doc's nobody's fool. He'll play this fair, but hard, you mark my word, but remember, I always have the last one. You'll see. Noon tomorrow.'

Harold Penney gulped. 'Easy enough to say.' He blinked. 'But, hell, you're the judge. I ain't so confident.' He fidgeted with his waistcoat. 'Mebbe pullin' out might be best. Leave town while there's still a chance.'

Slaney glanced quickly at Horan, his expression taut, the merest hint of a question in his eyes.

'That's fool talk, Harold,' growled the judge. 'If you've that in mind you should have done it long back. Too late now.'

The sheriff lit a cheroot and narrowed a tight, consuming stare behind the smoke.

Cassie walked the length of the veranda at the rear of Doc Sims's clapboard house, paused a moment to stare at the high moon and the sprinkling of stars in the black night sky, and struck a clenched fist on the rail in front of her.

'Damnit,' she hissed, 'I know you're right – know it as well as I know that's the moon up there – but, hell, it scares me, and that's no foolin'.'

Doc Sims turned the glass of whiskey in his hand with a thoughtful motion, watched the swirl of liquid, then downed the measure in one.

'Me too, if I'm honest,' he said, 'but I can't stand back and watch this happen. I just can't find it in me. So,' he gestured with the empty glass, 'somethin's got to be done, and I'm the somebody doin' it.'

Cassie turned and walked back slowly to where the

doc stood in shadow beyond the pool of moonlight.

'You're takin' one almighty risk, but you don't need me to tell you that. Horan and the others are for havin' this buried once and for all. They want a hangin' more than the townfolk – and I don't figure Judge Bream for lettin' this chance slip through his fingers.' She paused to tease the frills on her dress. 'You spoken to the fella yet?'

'Couple of minutes. That's all Horan would allow until he marched him back to jail. Said I could see him first thing in the mornin'. I'll be there.'

'What you goin' to ask him?'

Sims placed the glass on a windowledge.

'Start with the obvious, I guess: who he is, where he's from, why on earth he's turned up here in Faithfull, and just where he was on June twenty-four.'

Cassie watched the night for a while before asking: 'Do you think he'll tell you?'

'Be a fool if he don't. Why do you ask?'

Cassie shrugged. 'Seein' him there tonight I kinda got the impression he's his own man, makes up his own mind and does whatever he's decided, no messin'. He wouldn't be for corralin' easy. And that bothers me some.'

'How come?'

'Well, if my figurin' is right, and it ain't usually that far lackin' when it comes to men, why did he let Sheriff Horan take him without so much as a hoot of protest, accordin' to Charlie Toon at the livery who saw it all? Why didn't he at least protest his inno-cence? Why didn't he make a run for it then and there? Hell, Horan's no sharp-shootin' gunslinger, and it takes Charlie the best part of his strength to fork muck, so where was the opposition to a man who, if he's really a drifter lookin' for the next chance to make a fast dollar or find anythin' worthwhile for nothin', could have cleared town in a matter of minutes?'

'And what do you think, Cassie?'

'I don't, not yet, I just keep askin' questions.' She laid a hand on Doc Sims's arm. 'What I do know, and what I ain't for arguin', is that you're goin' to need some help over this – and I'm volunteerin'. And besides, you need me. I already know a deal about that night, and I reckon for there bein' a whole lot more to be heard.'

'I'm grateful to you, Cassie, but Slaney ain't goin' to like it. You know how he feels about you.'

Cassie brushed angrily at the folds of her long dress.

'Slaney can go do as he pleases. I know what I'm doin', and that's for final. Now, if you've got a measure of that whiskey goin' spare, I'll join you while we get to plannin'. . . .'

A rooster had already crowed loud and clear and the first smudge of grey light had broken in the eastern skies when Cassie slipped back to her room at Slaney's bar by the rear door and Doc Sims made his way down the deserted street to the sheriff's office.

Horan was waiting. 'Ain't wastin' any time, are you,' he said, pouring fresh coffee from the pot into two mugs. 'Guess you could use one of these, eh?'

Sims thanked him as he gazed anxiously beyond

the sheriff's shoulders to the dark shadows of the cells.

'How's Quarry?' he asked, sampling the steaming coffee.

'Still sleepin' last time I looked. He's a cool enough customer now. Might be a whole sight different story once we get to the business and he realizes how close that noose is gettin'.'

Sims said nothing, his gaze still fixed on the silent cells.

' 'T'ain't too late, you know,' Horan continued watchfully. 'You could still pull out. Ain't nobody goin' to think any the worse of you. And let's face it, Doc, is the fellow worth it? Hell, what is he? A two-bit drifter; rootless, homeless, not a cent to his name, scroungin' and stealin' wherever and whenever he gets the chance. Territory's lousy with 'em. Frankly, I'm—'

'Shall we begin?' said Sims, replacing the mug on the table. 'Time's short, and there's a lot to be done.'

Horan gritted his teeth.

'Waste of time,' he hissed, collecting the cell keys from a drawer in his desk. 'You'll live to regret this, Doc. You surely will.'

CHAPTER SIX

'Why you doin' this?' John Quarry stared intently through the half shadowed, half dawn-lit gloom of the cell, the nerve in his cheek settling quietly, his body relaxed against the bleak wall at his back.

'A whole heap of reasons it'd take too long to spell out in the time we've got,' said Doc Sims quickly, his tone levelled but intense. 'But principally because I ain't for seein' an innocent man go to a hangin' to save the necks of others.'

'You don't know I'm innocent.'

Doc's gaze tightened. 'Mister, I *know*. Take that as read. Now, you are who you say, aren't you – John Quarry?'

The man nodded.

'And you are from Wyoming?'

'Born there. Left when I was fifteen. Pa trailed the family to Colorado. When he died and Ma soon followed, I pulled out.'

Doc grunted. 'To where?'

'Most places. Utah, Kansas. Spent some time out St Louis way; rode the Big Muddy steamers, that sort of thing.'

'Doin' what? How'd you pay your way?'

Quarry's blue eyes seemed to ice over.

'I made out.'

Sims grunted again. He was learning fast: you could feel the chill, hear the doors clang shut in your mind when the man had said all he was going to say.

'And when precisely did you hit the Panflats?'

'Four days back,' said Quarry flatly, his eyes unblinking.

'Four days ago . . .' pondered Sims. 'Four days . . . But from where? Where had you travelled from?'

'South. Been holed up a time at a Mexican town name of Sercovista. Drifted north again late spring.'

'Drifted,' repeated Doc pointedly. 'You drifted into the Panflats?'

'Just that, Doc. No more, no less.'

'Headin' where?'

The blue eyes iced again.

'No place special. Figured I'd take a look at Faithfull, then move on when it suited.'

'I see,' murmured Sims quietly. 'A pity you made that choice. But you did. You're here and what's happened has happened. Now all we've got to do—'

'You all through there, Doc?' called Horan from his office. 'Me and my deputy got a busy day comin' up. Prisoner's got to be fed and watered, and there's town matters demandin' my attention, and you know how Judge Bream's a real stickler for time when he's sittin' a court, so mebbe you should move, eh?'

Doc sighed and adjusted his hat.

'Hmmm . . . seems like they've decided I've outstayed my welcome. But thanks, and I'll see you at noon. Meantime, say nothin'.'

The man's eyes followed Sims to the door. The nerve in his cheek twitched once and then was still.

Harold Penney had been up since the rooster crowed. And busy. He had gone to some trouble packing the saddle-bags with the items he considered essential for immediate survival and longer term for the fresh start he planned.

Clothes would be needed, but he had been selective, nothing heavy, nothing bulky. The tools of his trade – his shaving and hairdressing kit, a couple of bottles of the fancy afters from back East — were vital. Hell, he had been barbering since a youth; swept store for old man Beedles out West at Middlerocks before setting up on his own in Faithfull. That had maybe not been such a good day. . . .

He broke the reverie and turned to counting out the money he would carry. As much as he could reasonably handle had been the initial thinking. But then he had got to reflecting; the sheer weight to be carried by one horse over some distance was fast growing. Pockets full of money and saddlebags tight with clothes were not going to be a heap of good fortune if he found himself stranded in the badlands with one exhausted horse and a hundred miles of dirt still to cross.

But water would – the priority of a second canteen – as would a decent weapon and a supply of ammunition. Now he was thinking straight. . . .

He would head north for the hills, then move

deep into the mountain ranges. He would be safe there for weeks. He had heard say as how a fellow could live for months in the rocks and pine forests of the foothills without seeing a soul, or needing to.

He would maybe do just that: stay low, out of sight, silent, just a shadow, till he figured it time to make the final push, find a small town some place, open a new shop, begin a new life, and put the misery of memories behind him. He could do it, of course he could.

Back to the packing. . . .

Sheriff Horan drew his deputy aside to the deepest shadows of his office once Doc Sims had left and crossed into the still-deserted street.

'You been to the livery?' he asked. 'What's Charlie sayin'?'

'He says as how Penney collected his mount and tack late last night,' said Johnson. 'Got it hitched and saddled up back of his shop right now. But he was about early. Been a light burnin' in his back room since before first light.'

Horan rubbed a hand over his stubbled chin.

'Right, that looks to be clear enough. Guess we now know for certain what Harold's got in mind. He's pullin' out, fast as he can. Well, we'll see.' He considered silently for a moment, his gaze narrowed and dark. 'Can't have a nervy tongue like Harold's on the loose, can we. Too dangerous, and Harold ain't exactly the type to be trusted real deep, is he. He fidgets, sweats, gets to sayin' things he shouldn't.'

'You got it, boss.' Johnson grinned through the

debris of broken, yellowed teeth. 'I hear your thinkin'. Leave it to me. We'll have poor Harold back in Faithfull in no time at all – in good time to bury him along of that Wyoming drifter there, eh?'

Horan relaxed. 'Do a good job, Frank. No bunglin', no mess. We need to keep the town on our side, moreso 'til we've got Quarry set for a hangin'.'

The deputy adjusted his hat, tightened his gunbelt a notch, then merely winked as he slid from the office like a hungry rattler to the gently breaking first light.

Cassie had been expecting the knock on the door. She just wondered why it had taken so long.

'What kept you?' she mocked, standing back to admit Otis Slaney to the softly lit room. 'You ain't usually so slow. Got somethin' on your mind, or did you have to consult your partners before makin' a move?'

Slaney closed the door quietly, leaned back on it and folded his arms.

'You've been busy,' he said, smoothing his moustache even at this early hour. 'Spent most of the night with Doc Sims, I'm told. And you weren't sharin' his bed.'

'You have eyes everywhere, Otis!' quipped Cassie, selecting a plain blue day-dress from her wardrobe. 'And what do you deduce from your sneaky observations?'

Slaney was thoughtful for a moment, as if selecting a line of stepping-stones.

'I'd figure for you plannin' to help Doc in this

39

mad scheme he's got to defend John Quarry.'

'Well, you'd be dead-eyed right,' Cassie smiled, turning to display the dress against her in the long mirror.

'And might I ask why?' said Slaney.

'Sure you can. It's simple enough. I just happen to share Doc's opinion that Quarry is deservin' of a fair trial for what he's charged with, and not, as seemed sure as hell certain last night, likely to find himself with a rope round his neck on the say-so of a handful of Faithfull's so-called upstandin' citizenry. Simple as that. Satisfied?' Cassie flounced the dress across her hips.

Slaney watched and waited before continuing darkly:

'That's a mite prickly ground you're treadin' there. 'T'ain't goin' to be much appreciated, specially by some of my free-spendin' customers. Could be damagin' to business, not to mention reputations.'

Cassie swung round, the blue dress flaring across her like a breaking wave.

'That a fact,' she snapped. 'Well, God bless us, ain't that just troublesome! Let me tell you somethin' about your free-spenders with reputations, they ain't no better than louse-ridden, dirt-smellin' sons-of-prairie-bitches with no hope and no manners deservin' of a whore's loose spit! Them's your special customers, and I don't give a damn!'

The saloon owner unfolded his arms and eased away from the door.

'You're talkin' big, Cassie. Just hope you know

what you're sayin'.'

'Believe me, mister, I ain't started yet,' snapped Cassie again. 'There's a whole heap of questions buzzin' through my head about what happened that night at the McCrindle spread – what *really* happened. And you know somethin', I'm of a mind to get some answers, and that mebbe goes for Doc too.'

The sudden silence between them thickened, stares deepened; Cassie fought to control her seething; Slaney fingered the twirled points of his moustache.

'You goin' to get into that dress?' he asked at last.

'You bet your sweet life I am,' clipped Cassie.

'Then do it,' smiled Slaney. 'I can wait.'

The clock in the saloon bar had clunked noisily to midday when Sheriff Horan rose to his feet, called the crowded gathering to order and made his formal announcement.

'This court's now in session, Judge Theodore Bream presidin'.'

The judge glared from the already smoke-hazed gloom, adjusted the angle of his derby and crashed his gavel to the table.

'You layin' out the prosecution here, Sheriff?' he croaked.

'That I am,' said Horan, glancing quickly at the prisoner.

'Then let's get on with it. Let's hear the worst.'

CHAPTER SEVEN

Harold Penney sweated, shielded his eyes against the fierce noon glare, licked his cracked lips and took a careful step through the burning Panflats dirt.

'That'll be far enough, Harold. Just stand well clear of your mount there, drop that gunbelt and don't move.'

He knew the voice. Of course he did.

'That you, Frank?' he croaked, the words as brittle as brushwood. 'What the hell you doin' out here?'

'Might ask the same of you, Harold.' Deputy Johnson smiled as he emerged from the rocky outcrop flanking the backdrop to the foothills and mountain peaks. 'Not much barberin' to be done today, eh? Takin' a break or somethin'?' The deputy's eyes narrowed as he levelled the drawn Colt in his hand. 'Wouldn't be leavin' town by any chance, would you?'

'What the hell you sayin' there, Frank?' Penney squirmed, his hands gesturing weakly. 'As if . . . Damnit, I ain't got no good reason to be pullin' out.'

'Well, we sure thought that, Harold, all of us – me,

the sheriff, Judge Bream, Marv and Otis. Got to stick together, ain't we. Can't be reckonin' now on splittin' up and goin' our own sweet ways, can we. Wouldn't be right.'

Johnson's smile slid to a leering grin. 'I been watchin' you since sun-up, Harold. I know all about you collectin' that mount last night from Charlie Toon's stables. I seen you packin' them saddle-bags, fixin' up that bedroll. Now that ain't the habit of a fella set to take a ride for the early mornin' air, is it?'

The sweat broke freely across the barber's brow.

'Heck, Frank, I just kinda got to thinkin' on things, needed some time on my own. You know how it is.'

'Oh, sure,' grinned Johnson with a mocking shrug of his shoulders. He was silent a moment, the grin fading. 'And just what sort of thinkin' would that be, Harold? Wouldn't have anythin' to do with what happened out at McCrindle's, would it? Wouldn't be concernin' that night? Don't tell me you're gettin' cold feet.'

Penney fidgeted, wiped the sweat from his face and screwed his aching eyes to slits.

'Think about it, Frank,' he began anxiously. 'Ain't no guarantee that fella Quarry's goin' to hang, is there? Specially not now Doc Sims is defendin' him. Hell, there ain't no sayin' to what might come out. Could be anythin', and there's no knowin' how deep it might go. We could all end up at the end of a rope.'

'You've sure got yourself worked up there some, Harold,' said Johnson. 'So you've figured for cuttin' loose while you've got the chance, eh? Fresh start some place. Clean sheet. No lookin' over your shoulder, no bad memories crowdin' every time you set foot on the Pan. That the way of it?'

'That's it, Frank.' Penney smiled. 'You've got it – and I'll tell you somethin', my friend, you could join me here. Damnit, I've got enough cash stashed in them saddle-bags for two of us, no problem. Enough to buy you a spread, Frank. Mebbe get to a little horse-breedin', eh? All the land you'd ever need up north there. And a good time on the way to go with it. What you say, Frank? What you reckon?'

'That's a mighty temptin' offer put like that, Harold, and, you know somethin', I'm real grateful to you for makin' it. But I think not.'

The grin had faded completely from Johnson's lips, the expression tightened, the eyes darkened to an unblinking stare.

'But I sure understand your need to be alone,' the deputy continued almost lightly. 'I see that. And seein' as how one good turn deserves another and how appreciative I am of your offer, I'm goin' to make you an offer you ain't goin' to be in no position to refuse – in a manner of speakin'. Ain't that decent of me?'

Two shots brought Harold Penney to his knees, clutching his bleeding gut; a third, close up, between the eyes, finished him.

Deputy Frank Johnson loaded the body on to the barber's mount and led it back to the trail to Faithfull. He would be there inside a couple of hours.

'I tell you straight up, same as I've said it many times,

44

that weren't no sight for any man to stomach.' Sheriff Horan paused in his long address, first to catch Judge Bream's eye to indicate a suitable silence for the gathering in the bar to feel the tension, secondly for the prisoner to maybe stir himself from that cold, unblinking stare he had held since being escorted from the jail.

'In your own time, Sheriff,' murmured the judge eventually, at the same time pouring himself a measure from a newly opened bottle. 'We ain't in no hurry.'

Doc Sims shifted in his chair impatiently. Cassie, at his side, laid a soft hand on his arm and whispered bitingly:

'Not all that again. This is the bit he enjoys.'

The crowded bar murmured under careful breath, anxious not to disturb, but desperate to say something. The bullock-chested man finished his drink and added to the thickening haze of smoke by lighting a cigar. A woman nearby spread a paper fan indignantly.

Otis Slaney watched Cassie from behind the bar, his gaze clear as a perched hawk's. A bar girl sniffed and dabbed a cloth at her running nose.

Marv Hinton adjusted his coat for the twentieth time, looked round him quickly and then, his puzzled frown deepening, at the batwings and the glare of sunlight beyond them. Where was Penney, he wondered?

His shop had not been opened; there had been no response to repeated knocking at the back door, and worse, no visible sign or sounds of a presence.

So just what in tarnation had the fool been getting up to? Trouble with Harold was he had a tendency to panic, lose any straight thinking he had, and this affair – the court, the prisoner – was just the sort of thing to go scattering his brains to the wind. If by any chance he had taken it on himself to . . .

'Herb McCrindle had been shot and was long dead by the time we got there. Just lyin' in a pool of blood; seemed like it stretched the whole length of the cabin.'

Horan waited, almost feeling the silence. Judge Bream cleared his throat appropriately.

'He'd been shot, point blank, three times. Died where he fell,' the sheriff continued. 'But that was not the worst we found, not by a long shot. It was what we came to when we got to the bunk rooms, two of 'em, that really churned the guts.'

'Let's just establish who was with you at this time, Sheriff,' said the judge, widening his bloodshot eyes. 'For the benefit of the folks here and, of course, Doc Sims. Don't want there to be no confusion, do we.'

Horan nodded. 'My deputy, Frank Johnson; Marv Hinton over at the store; Harold Penney and Otis Slaney. Just the five of us.'

'How come?' said Sims, jumping to his feet. 'How come all five of you were out there that night? Mite unusual, weren't it?'

Judge Bream banged the gavel to the table amid a sudden surge of murmuring.

'Let's have some order here,' he boomed. 'Silence in court.' He glared at Doc Sims. 'Your turn to put questions will come, Doc. But in the meantime—'

'But it's a fair point, your Honour,' pursued Sims with an exaggerated emphasis on the 'Honour'. 'I mean, how often does that happen, or is it a regular habit among these men? Do they ride out to the Pan as a matter of some civic duty I ain't yet heard of, or were they out there that night for their health? And while I'm on my feet, your Honour, how come it was close on two hours before Deputy Johnson roused me?'

The saloon-bar gathering shuffled restlessly, the murmuring grew louder until the bullock-chested man pushed back his chair and came to his feet.

'Doc's right there, Judge,' he called above the continuing babble. 'Prisoner's deservin' of an answer. Won't make no odds, but right's right.'

Judge Bream crashed his gavel to the table again.

'I don't need you, mister, to remind me of what's right in my court. Now you just sit yourself down before I charge you with contempt.' He reached for the whiskey bottle, poured a measure and sank it in a single gulp. He turned his bleary stare on Horan. 'Well, Sheriff, you goin' to answer so we can all get on?'

'Sure I am.' The sheriff smiled. 'There's no mystery involved.'

'Liar,' hissed Cassie, glancing quickly at Sims.

'Fact of it is,' began Horan with a confident sweep of his gaze over the assembled townfolk, 'that Frank Johnson, Marv Hinton, Harold Penney, Otis Slaney and myself had been in conversation with Herb McCrindle over the possibility of Faithfull setting up its first town committee, a sort of council with everyone's interests and well-bein' at heart. Herb, we figured, would be a good representative of our outlyin' homesteaders. That night we were on our way to another meetin' with him.'

'First I've heard of any such committee,' hissed Cassie again.

'As to why, by Doc's reckonin', it took two hours for Frank Johnson to raise him,' the sheriff went on, addressing the gathering directly, 'well, now, I ask you, folks, is that so surprisin'? Hell, we'd just ridden into the bloodbath of a massacre. We'd none of us ever seen anythin' like it. We were stunned out of our minds, heads reelin'; we couldn't think for the stench and the sights of death. Is it any wonder it took time for Frank to pull himself together suffi-cient to ride back to town to raise Doc? I think not. Ain't a man breathin' who'd have felt any different.'

Horan's gaze hardened and blackened like a sudden night.

'We were standin' witness to the work of a crazed beast on that night.' He swung round, his arm outstretched, finger pointing. 'The work of that man – John Quarry.'

CHAPTER EIGHT

'This ain't lookin' good,' grimaced Cassie, taking another turn round her room, pausing at the foot of the bed to lay a hand on Sims's shoulder before moving to the window. 'Horan's gettin' it all his own way.' She fumbled with the unlit cheroot in her fingers, thought about lighting it, then tossed it angrily on to her dressing-table. 'Town committee my backside!' she scoffed. 'There ain't no such thinkin' goin' on. Never has been. Never will be. Horan and Judge Bream run this town between them. Always have.'

Doc slapped his hands to his knees.

'That's as mebbe,' he said, his face tense behind the tiredness and drawn, uncertain pallor, 'but they can't be allowed to get away with this, not nohow they can't. There weren't no excuse for all the time that passed before Frank Johnson raised me that night. And I know exactly what's comin' next – he's goin' to tell Judge Bream, the whole town, as how Herb McCrindle's wife said a few words before she finally died. He'll swear on the Bible that she whispered somethin' about a fella with pale, ice-blue eyes who definitely said the word Wyoming.'

Doc stood up, stretched and crossed to the small corner table where he poured two drinks, He handed one to Cassie. 'I can hear him now, hear him sayin' it, and if Quarry's eyes had been brown, or green, Louise McCrindle would have whispered brown or green, same as she'd have whispered Texas, Kansas or any other doggone place if it so suited. The whole thing's a cover-up for the real truth.'

'And just what is the truth?' asked Cassie, staring into the shadow-streaked glare of the street.

Doc sighed, his gaze lost in the slow swirl of the drink in the glass.

'I think we're both of the same mind, Cassie,' he said quietly. 'I think we both know that the five men out there on the Pan that night were responsible for the deaths of McCrindle, his wife, and daughter Alice. How that came about is beyond me right now, but it's the only explanation I can find based on what I saw when I got to the home and what I know instinctively in my bones. What is an absolute, rock-solid certainty is that John Quarry was nowhere near the place. There was more than one man involved in the rapin' – and I'll stake my neck he wasn't one of them.'

Sims finished the drink quickly and reached for his jacket on the chair at his side. 'Trouble is, of course, we ain't got a whisker of proof.'

'Well, there's one source of it you ain't never goin' to get to questionin',' said Cassie, stepping closer to the window. 'Take a look at this.'

'Where'd you find him?' asked Doc Sims, peering closer to examine the body of Harold Penney slung like a bag of beans across his horse. The town crowd, spilling from Slaney's saloon to the street, pressed forward to satisfy their own curiosities.

'Out on the Pan, someways short of the Freeman spread,' said Deputy Johnson, dusting the dirt from his shirt and pants.

'He's been shot,' croaked a man at the front of the crowd.

'Harold's been shot, folks. Yuh can see it right here. All that dried blood.'

'Who the hell'd want to go shootin' somebody like Harold Penney, f'cris'sake?' said another, spitting between his boots. 'Darned fool wouldn't have harmed a fly.'

'What in tarnation was he doin' out there, anyhow?' asked an older man, scratching his beard.

Doc Sims turned to the deputy. 'Any ideas?'

'None,' shrugged Johnson, conscious of Sheriff Horan moving to his side. 'Found him just like you see. No saddle-bags, no bedroll, nothin'. So it don't seem like he was going far. Mebbe just takin' a mornin' ride. Somebody must have seen him – mebbe another of them driftin' types – and figured he was easy pickin's.'

'But what did his killer take?' said the old man, still scratching. 'Damnit, he even left his horse. So what was the point?'

Doc stared intently at Johnson whose mouth had opened, but his voice stayed silent in his darting glance to Horan.

'Well, ain't no sayin' to how it happened right now, is there,' said the sheriff, beginning to urge the crowd back to the bar. 'But don't you fret, folks, me and Frank'll be lookin' into it just as soon as we've got the matter of the trial cleared up. Meantime, ease off there for now and get back to your seats. Judge Bream'll be callin' the court to order shortly. We'll take care of Harold 'til we can bury him decent.'

The town men murmured among themselves, shuffled to the cooler shade of the boardwalk, lingered at the batwings, some still glancing anxiously back to the body, some licking their lips at the prospect of drinks.

'This way, boys.' Slaney beamed, pushing open the 'wings invitingly. 'Still time to take some refreshment before the judge resumes. Credit is approved for the day, and the girls are . . . let's say bein' more than sociable. Step this way.' He curled his waxed moustache and nodded quickly in Horan's direction.

'Bad business, Doc,' said the sheriff. 'But thanks, anyhow, for what you did.'

'Precisely nothin',' murmured Sims. 'Penney's been dead some time. Well before noon. If he'd reached the Freeman spread, he must have left early and ridden hard. He was shot, I'd reckon, at close range. Point blank.'

Horan stiffened his shoulders.

'Yeah, like I say, a bad business. Still . . .'

'What was Frank doin' out there?' clipped Sims sharply.

'Doin'?' frowned Horan. 'Well, now, he was doin' what keepin' the law is all about, Doc. He was out checkin' things.'

'Checkin' out things? What things? And why that

52

far out? Damnit, you're three-quarters to the pines by the time you get to the Freeman's place.'

Horan stiffened again, his gaze darkening.

'Just so.' He waited, the thoughts tumbling behind the stare. 'There's been reports of some horse-thievin' out that way. Frank was just takin' a look round. There's nothin' definite, but it pays to be careful, don't it.'

Sims held the sheriff's stare for some moments.

'Like you say, pays to be careful. I'll remember that.'

'They're all lyin', all of them about everythin'. It's all lies.' Cassie flounced into the chair at Sims's side and gazed angrily round the crowded, smoke-hazed bar where already some early evening lanterns had been lit. 'And now, I suppose we're goin' to hear a whole heap more.'

'Easy,' said Sims, taking Cassie's hand. 'Ain't nothin' we can do right now, save go along with what-ever the judge there dictates.'

Cassie stared defiantly ahead. 'Frank Johnson's lyin' through his teeth,' she simmered, the words hissing on her breath like steam. 'Harold Penney was pullin' out, you can bet to it.'

'He was travellin' light if that's the case.'

Cassie's lips tightened. 'I'd wager a hidin' to nothin' that Frank stripped down the mount before he trailed it in. Probably got Penney's belongin's stashed somewhere back at his place.'

'Well . . .' Doc sighed.

'I'm right, I know I am,' said Cassie, breaking the stare. 'Harold was one of the five out on the Pan that night. He knew well enough what happened, then he got cold feet and tried to make a run for it. But Horan was ahead of him and Frank Johnson was waitin'. And that's the top and bottom of it.' Her eyes were suddenly wide and bright in their gaze into Sims's face. 'Good as a confession, ain't it?'

'But what we don't know—' began Doc.

Judge Bream's gavel crashed to the table.

'Quiet out there,' he called, his jowls shaking, a shimmer of old cigar ash drifting from his waistcoat. 'Guess I know what you're all thinkin' and turnin' your minds to. Shootin' of our good friend and fellow citizen, Harold Penney, is a heinous crime, one you can bet your boots Sheriff Horan and his representatives of the law hereabouts will investigate thoroughly and subsequently bring to justice the evil perpetrators.'

'Sonofa-lyin'-bitch,' hissed Cassie.

'Meantime,' continued the judge above the subdued murmurings of the saloon-bar gathering, 'this court, myself presidin', is in session again.' He poured a measure from the half-empty bottle and sank it quickly. 'Sheriff Horan will resume his account of what he found out at the McCrindle home that night – and keep it brief as he can. Time's pressin'.'

'Certainly, your Honour,' said Horan coming to his feet. 'And may I say that I join wholeheartedly in condemnation of the shootin' today of Harold Penney.' He waited, glanced round the watching faces, then cleared his throat.

'Louise McCrindle was clingin' on to life by a thread when we got to her,' he began.

'You bet she was!' mouthed Cassie.

54

'She was in a terrible state. There was blood and—'

'Spare us the details, Sheriff,' croaked the judge. 'Just stick to the facts.'

'Sure,' said Horan, stiffening.

'Did Mrs McCrindle say anythin'? That's the nub of it.'

'Yes, your Honour, she did.'

A buzz of murmuring swept through the bar. Judge Bream's gavel banged again.

'Silence in court,' he ordered. 'Get to it, Sheriff.'

'The words she spoke were faint, but heard clear enough by myself, Marv Hinton and Otis Slaney.' Horan paused again. 'She said somethin' about icy eyes, a man with ice-blue eyes; she faltered a moment and then said, plain as the wind, the word Wyoming. No doubt about it. She said Wyoming.'

The gathering erupted into raised voices, the bite of scraping chairs.

'That settles it then, don't it,' shouted someone at the back of the bar. 'That's the fella. The prisoner!'

Judge Bream called for silence, his gavel raised, eyes flashing.

'Silence I say!' The gavel crashed. He waited, glaring. 'That'll be it for the day.'

'But hold on there, Judge,' called Doc Sims, springing to his feet, Cassie at his side. 'I've got a right here, to question the sheriff on what we've just heard, and I insist on exercisin' it.'

'Insist all you like, Doc,' the judge glowered, 'but this court is now adjourned. We'll continue proceedin's tomorrow, sharp at noon.'

'Sons-of-goddamn-lyin'-two-bit-bitches!' swore Cassie above the crowing of excited voices and jostling bodies.

CHAPTER NINE

'You should ease up there some, Doc. 'T'ain't the end of the world.' Marv Hinton adjusted the set of the tied cravat at his neck and dusted the lapels of his frock-coat yet again.

'Sure goin' to be the end of John Quarry's world if somebody don't stand to justice for the fella, ain't it.' Sims thrust his hands into the pockets of his pants and stared into the deepening night from the veranda of his home.

'You're right on that score, sure you are,' said the storekeeper, watching the doc carefully, 'and there wouldn't be a man not agree – hell, there but for the grace of God, eh? – but, damn it, Doc, you heard what Sheriff Horan told Judge Bream, that was plain enough. Couldn't have been clearer, leastways not by my reckonin'.'

Sims held his stare on the night for another ten long seconds, the words he wanted to speak tight behind clenched teeth.

'You here for a purpose, Marv,' he forced himself to ask at last, 'or just takin' the air?'

Hinton smiled condescendingly.

'No ulterior motives here, Doc. Ain't tryin' to influence the defence or anythin' like that! No, it was just that the sheriff, myself and Otis got to thinkin' that, what with the trial and now the shootin' of Harold Penney, well it kinda occurred to us—'

'What do you know of this so-called town council Horan was speakin' of?' snapped Doc suddenly.

'How do you mean, what do I know?' Hinton frowned.

'Just that – what do you know? First I'd heard of it 'til Horan raised it. How long had it been planned, on whose say-so, and why? And why a meetin' with McCrindle at that hour out there on the Pan? Why not invite McCrindle to town, and why had he not said anythin' of it before? Hell, I was talkin' to him right there in the street two days before he died. Why didn't you have your *meeting* with him then?'

'I ain't followin' precisely what you're gettin' at here, Doc,' flustered Hinton, fiddling with the cravat again.

'Oh but I think you are, Marv,' persisted Sims. 'I think you know exactly what I'm sayin': there weren't no plans for no town council, committee, call it what you will. There never had been. That was a whole ramblin' fiction concocted by Horan.' His stare came alight like a primed lamp. 'Right, aren't I? Horan was lyin' there today. So why were the five of you out at the McCrindle place that night? There has to be a reason, Marv.'

A fine beading of sweat glistened on the store-keeper's brow.

'I don't have to listen to this,' he shuddered, hands flapping at the folds of his coat. 'I came here tonight in a spirit of friendship and a sense of our civic duty to stay together and to ask . . . Well, it don't matter none now. If you want to query anythin' Sheriff Horan said today, then I suggest you ask him face to face.'

'Don't you fret about that, Marv, I sure as hell will!' Hinton drew himself to his full, tailored height.

'Meantime, I'd be a whole lot careful where I was treadin' if I were you, Doc. You might get to nosin' at things that don't concern you.'

The flame in the lantern hanging from the veranda ceiling flickered in the shift of a drifting breeze. Sims's eyes narrowed.

'You threatenin' me, Marv?'

'I ain't threatenin' you, 'course I ain't. Why should I? I've got nothin' to hide.' Hinton swallowed and turned his neck against a sudden tightness of the cravat. 'All I'm sayin' to you is—'

'Did Harold Penney have somethin' to hide?' clipped Doc. 'That why he pulled out like he did?'

'No, not Harold. Damn it, Doc, you knew him as well as any of us. Harold was as jumpy, as unpredictable as a flushed jack rabbit in spring. Never no sayin' to what he was thinkin', or might do. I guess he just took it into his head this mornin' to saddle up and ride out to the Pan, no sayin' what for. That was Harold.'

'And there just happened to be a passin' gunslinger loungin' out there, doin' nothin', mindin' his own business, 'til Harold happened along and offered himself as a target. Same as there just happened to be a no-hope drifter passin' the McCrindle place who took a shine to the good-lookin' Mrs McCrindle and who then, would you believe, had the decency to show up right here in town.' Sims ran a hand over his florid face. 'That's just the sort of thing that happens here in Faithfull, ain't it, Marv? Should rename the place Coincidence!'

'There you go again, makin' one almighty mountain out of—'

The crack of fast shots from a blazing Colt rang out across the night like something being shattered to destruction in the high heavens.

'What in the name of—'

'Them shots were fired at the jail,' croaked Sims. 'Come on!'

'I'll kill that woman, so help me I will, with my own bare hands!' Sheriff Horan thundered from his office to the boardwalk and stared like a man possessed at the sea of faces watching him from the shadowy, lantern-lit darkness of the night. 'And just what in hell do you want?'

'Plain enough, Sheriff,' shouted the bullock-chested man from the front of the throng. 'We want to know what's happened.' Supporting voices urged him on. 'Is it true that Quarry's escaped?'

'It's true,' said Horan reluctantly, hands clamped to his hips. 'He's escaped. Somehow managed to get hold of a gun. Shot his way out, but there ain't nobody hit bad, save Deputy Johnson, who's nursin' a sore head.'

A wiry old-timer smacked his lips and sucked noisily on a corn-cob pipe. 'How'd yuh mean: *managed to
get hold of a gun?* What yuh sayin' there?' The crowd
jeered and mocked.

'Means somebody gave him one, that's what he
means!' cracked a youth, shoving his hat to the back
of his head.

'So who gave him a gun?' bellowed bullock-chest
above the shouts.

The crowd fell silent, eyes fixed on the sheriff.

'We ain't sure yet,' lied Horan, glancing quickly at
Frank Johnson as he moved uncertainly to the boardwalk, a blood-soaked rag pressed tight to the wound
at his temple. 'Frank here didn't get a clear view of
the person involved – but you ain't got no reason to
fret. We'll have that sonofabitch back behind bars in
no time.'

'Not if he's got a horse you won't,' smacked the
old-timer. 'I hear as how he had a horse waitin' on
him. That so?'

'He had a horse,' conceded Horan. 'But don't ask
me who tacked it up and brought it to the back of the
jail. I don't know yet, so I suggest – in fact, I'm
orderin' – you all to clear the street right now. You
either go home or you go take a drink at Slaney's.
One or the other.' He released his hands from his
hips. 'Just do it, you hear?'

The old-timer grumbled and spat. The youth
replaced his hat and coughed on an intake of cheroot
smoke. The bullock-chested man hesitated, glared
directly into Horan's eyes, the silence between the
two men as threatening as a stray keg of dynamite.

'Suggest you don't waste no time, Sheriff,' said the man. 'That fella could be dangerous, specially now he's loose.'

'Let's do like the sheriff says, shall we?' said Sims, easing from the shadows with Marv Hinton at his side. 'Ain't no more to be done here tonight. Let the sheriff get to his work, and give me some space to tend to Deputy Johnson.'

The gathering murmured darkly, glanced back at the sheriff, but shuffled slowly, grudgingly towards the lights of the saloon where a group of bar girls under Slaney's direction decorated the boardwalk and batwings.

'And now,' said Doc Sims bluntly, turning to face the sheriff, 'let's hear the real story of what's happened to John Quarry – the man I'm supposed to be defendin' on a charge of rape and murder. I take it you do know?'

CHAPTER TEN

'She did it, no doubtin' to it, and she'll pay. Oh, brother, how she'll pay!' Horan prowled like a mangy lion round his office, a fist thudding into the palm of his hand, his shadow lunging, eyes gleaming. 'She's a bitch, ain't no other word for her.'

Doc Sims stepped back from bandaging Frank Johnson's head and surveyed his handiwork with a satisfied grunt.

'You'll do,' he said. 'Just a bad headache.'

The deputy winced and helped himself to another shot of whiskey.

'Changes things some, don't it?' Doc ran his hands through a towel. 'Trial's postponed, I guess.'

'But that scumbag will be back in my hands faster than you can spit, Doc. Mark my word. I ain't for bein' made to look a fool. And as for that woman . . .' Horan kicked violently at the wall. 'Cassie, of all people. How the hell could she? Frank saw her, clear as day. Crept up on him. Hit him. Took the keys and freed Quarry. Why, in God's name?'

'Justice,' said Sims quietly, laying aside the towel

62

then reaching for his jacket. 'Mebbe she'd got to this crazy notion that Quarry wasn't gettin' a fair trial, was never goin' to get a fair trial, and mebbe she just reckoned on givin' the fella the only chance he was ever goin' to get in this town. Mebbe Cassie's idea of justice was the only option left to her: she sprang the fella, found the guts and courage to do it.' He slid tiredly into the jacket. 'I wouldn't advise seekin' to wreak your anger on Cassie, Sheriff. Won't do no good, and in any case you'll have me to reckon with. My advice would be to watch your back in case that driftin' fella decides to hang about awhile.'

'What the hell talk is that, Doc?' said the store-keeper, turning from the window. 'You sayin' as how Quarry won't make a run for it?'

'Mebbe he will, mebbe he won't.' Sims shrugged 'Who's to know right now. Most men would; head for the mountains and hole up long as it takes for the heat to cool. But, in my brief acquaintance with the fella, Quarry ain't most men. And more to the point, he ain't guilty as charged.'

Horan stepped to the whiskey bottle on his desk, pulled the tin mug from Johnson's grip, and poured a generous double measure for himself.

'I should throw you behind bars for talk like that, Doc.' He drank greedily at the whiskey. 'Keep you out of sight and silent.'

'To what end?' Sims shrugged again. 'Wouldn't serve no purpose, would it? We're all back to where we began: the McCrindle family was abused and murdered on the night of June twenty-fourth, and their killers are still walkin' free. Them's the facts,

Sheriff. No hidin' from them. And Cassie don't figure in them nohow.'

We'll see,' said Horan, finishing the drink. 'Meantime—'

'Meantime,' Sims smiled, reaching the door, 'you've still to find the killer of Harold Penney before you start hell-raisin' the Pans in search of Quarry. I'll bid you all goodnight.'

Sheriff Horan, Marv Hinton and Deputy Frank Johnson watched in silence as Doc Sims walked into the night.

Sims crossed quickly from the sheriff's office to the comparative glare and clamour of Slaney's bar. The street was deserted, but the saloon was doing brisk business, some men arguing vehemently over the comings and goings of the day, others debating more soberly the bewildering twists and turns of events since the stranger had ridden into town and so unexpectedly and easily escaped from it.

Sims paused for a moment in the shadows at the batwings, catching at the snatches of conversation that drifted above the clink of bottles and glasses.

'. . . he had help. Must have. How else do you get to unlockin' a cell door, walkin' out, with a loaded Colt and findin' your horse all conveniently saddled up and waitin' on you? Tell me that. That's help, and from somebody right here in town . . .'

'. . . Charlie Toon ain't sayin' nothin', save to keep repeatin' over and over that he never heard a thing, that somebody sneaked into the livery there and took Quarry's mount, saddle, the lot, just like that . . .'

'. . . mebbe Charlie's in on it, but who's he workin' with, f'cris'sake?'

'. . . Harold Penney was a darned sight shiftier than most would reckon to. Could see it in his eyes . . .'

'. . . supposin' Quarry comes back. Hell, imagine that . . .'

'. . . Quarry's got any sense he'll keep goin', faster than a streak of lightnin' . . .'

'. . . he was as guilty as any man I've ever seen. We should be havin' a hangin' here tonight. Quarry should be swingin' at the end of a rope . . .'

'. . . damn it, never figured I'd live to see this town get to where it is. Know somethin', there's bones rattlin' in corners ain't never been reckoned before, and don't you fret, there'll be ghosts walkin' soon enough. You bet . . .'

Only the squeals and giggles of a bar girl suggested that not everyone was concerning himself with the prospect of ghosts.

Sims glanced briefly into the crowded bar, established that Slaney was fully occupied taking money, and moved away to the deeper shadows along the alley to the rear of the saloon. He was trusting to the proprietor's long-established habit of leaving a back door open to gain him access to the stairs to Cassie's room.

Two minutes later his knock and whispered identification saw him standing in the shadowy, low-lit gloom of her private quarters, the drapes part drawn at the window, the bed covered with a scattered collection of clothes, boots, bottles of scent and a lacquered box of trinkets, brooches, rings, bangles, necklets and baubles.

'What the hell's goin' on here?' he frowned, watching as Cassie busied herself with the belongings.

'What's it look like?' she snapped, throwing aside a worn, faded dress. 'Sorry, didn't mean to bite your head off, but I'm pushin' time here, Doc. Thought for a minute you were Slaney, or worse, Horan. But they'll be here. Sure to be.' She examined another dress with a look of disdain. 'Hell, what do I need this for, f'cris'sake?'

'You're pullin' out?' said Sims.

'That's it. Pullin' right out. Faithfull ain't never goin' to see me again, not that they'll want to when they get to hearin' how I sprung John Quarry.'

Doc crossed quietly to the window and studied the empty street.

'How'd you manage that?' he asked.

'Easy enough. Charlie Toon owes me, and, like yourself, ain't so taken with Horan's way of goin' on, and he certainly ain't for the hangin' of an innocent man. He knew the risks, but he went along with me and reckoned it worth it. As for Frank Johnson – well, that took a bit of stomachin' on my part, but, when you get to the grit of it, he's a man, ain't he, just like the rest. He weren't no problem for as long as it took.'

Cassie discarded another dress. 'Should've said somethin' to you about what I was plannin', I know that, but you wouldn't have gone along with it. You were still holdin' to speakin' up for the fella at the trial, weren't you? Still are, I guess. But there weren't never goin' to be no justice for John Quarry. You know that as well as I do, Doc. And you're of the same mind as me as to who's really carryin' the guilt. The shootin' of Harold Penney proves that.'

She came to the doc's side and placed an arm across his shoulders. 'Sorry I went behind your back, but I ain't one bit sorry for what I did.'

Sims sighed and permitted himself a quiet smile.

'Mebbe you did the right thing. Fella's free now. Did he say anythin'?'

'Not a word,' said Cassie, returning to the cluttered bed. 'Weren't really the time or the occasion for a conversation. He just looked, nodded, said thanks, and went. I made myself scarce fast as I could. Frank meantime had recovered and was firin' shots like it was a hoedown. Locked myself in here and ain't moved since.'

Sims was silent for a moment, his thoughts spinning, his gaze flat on the mound of clothes and jewellery.

'You won't get clear of town, Cassie,' he said quietly. 'They won't let you. Horan'll be watchin' you like a hawk.'

'Goin' to have to take my chance,' said Cassie from behind a dress as she held it up for inspection. 'Do the best I can. Charlie says as how he'll fix a horse for me. Few supplies, water, some clothes, and I'll be gone.'

'And you won't get a half-mile before Horan's on to you. In any case, where you figurin' on headin'?'

Cassie lowered the dress.

'Ain't decided. Make for the hills first, then

67

mebbe . . . Hell, I don't know. There ain't been the time to reckon on it that close.'

Sims turned back to the window.

'This ain't the way, Cassie,' he murmured. 'But there is a better one.'

'Oh, and what might that be? I ain't seein' it, not after what's happened here tonight and with me plumb at the centre of it all.'

'Stay here in Faithfull. Help me bring to book them responsible for what happened that night.' Sims swung round from his view of the empty street, his gaze fixed and penetrating. 'We've made a start. John Quarry gave us that chance. Now let's finish it. You and me.'

Cassie threw the dress across the bed.

'You serious there, Doc?'

'Never been more serious. And it can be done.'

'But how? Like you've said, I'm a marked woman. What use am I goin' to be? And how's just the two of us goin' to stand against the likes of Horan? We ain't no gunslingin' duo, Doc. They'll have the pair of us behind bars faster than we can blink.'

Sims rubbed his chin. 'I reckon not. Horan's a mite confused at the moment. The town's restless, he don't know what's happened to Quarry or where he might have headed. Should he raise a posse and give chase, or does he leave it, let the fella go and concentrate on calmin' the town men? And what about Harold Penney? He's goin' to have to explain that before much longer. And then there's me.'

Sims paused to smile softly. 'I've become a problem because I ain't lettin' the McCrindle killin' rest, and for what I tried to do for Quarry. Town is part-ways with me. They want justice for a murdered family, even if they ain't sure at the moment where to look for it. Point is, Horan can't afford right now to take me off the street, and that's your insurance. Stick along of me and we can see this through.'

Cassie waited, staring at Sims and then at the clutter on the bed.

'What in tarnation do I need with all this?' She rummaged among the clothes, found a pair of pants and some cotton shirts and set them aside.

'Give me ten minutes and I'm with you!' She grinned, beginning to undress.

CHAPTER ELEVEN

Judge Bream sank his fourth whiskey from the newly opened bottle, belched, smacked his lips and drew on the cigar until the tip was glowing red.

'Let 'em go,' he said. 'We ain't got no choice at this moment.'

Horan grunted, listened to the babble and clatter of the crowded bar beyond the gloom of Slaney's back room, then sank wearily into a chair at the baize-topped table.

'Just like that,' he said, clicking his fingers. 'That two-bit whore empties my jail easy as spittin' on dirt, and we let her get away with it. Help yourself; take a chunk out of my deputy's head, grab the keys, open the cell and invite the prisoner to walk free! Looks good, don't it.'

' 'T'ain't quite like that,' soothed Marv Hinton from the far side of the room. 'Cassie's a clever woman. She knows how to work these things.'

' 'Course she does.' Slaney smiled, standing with his back to the door. 'It's what she's paid for, ain't it. She's one of the best. That's why she works for me.'

'But for how much longer?' grunted Horan.

'Chances are she won't be back here in no hurry.'

Slaney pinched the ends of his waxed moustache.

'Wouldn't take bets on that, Sheriff,' he murmured cynically.

'She'll stick with Doc,' said the judge, peering through a cloud of smoke. 'And that's fine by us. We'll always know where she is, what she's doin', what the pair of 'em together might get to doin'. You'll be able to take them any time of your choosin', Sheriff, and that's precisely how you want things. You're still in control.'

'Well said, Judge.' The storekeeper beamed. 'You're dead right there.'

'And Quarry, what about him?' asked Horan.

'He might be a different proposition.' The judge poured another measure from the bottle, examined the tip of his cigar, turning it slowly through his fingers. 'I don't reckon any one of us – and that includes Doc Sims – havin' anythin' like the level of the fella. We none of us know him, and he weren't givin' nothin' away.'

'He'll be into the hills come sun-up,' said Slaney, confidently. 'We ain't goin' to see him again.'

'How sure can you be?' murmured Hinton. 'Supposin'—'

'There ain't no supposin' to it,' persisted Slaney. 'He'll ride, and fast. Put this town long behind him. He got lucky, didn't he. He ain't goin' to push his luck again.'

'Even so, I'm still goin' to have to raise a posse,' said Horan, coming to his feet. 'Got to make this look somethin' like credible.'

Silence fell between the four. Judge Bream blew smoke. Slaney tended his moustache. Marv Hinton picked specks of dust from his frock-coat. Horan stared into the night beyond the window. The town men continued to fill the bar with their babble. It was the storekeeper who spoke first.

'Nearly had this buttoned up, didn't we. Hadn't been for Cassie gettin' suddenly so high-minded, about things . . . Hell, since when has she ever got to moralizin', 'specially where men are concerned. If I had my way—'

'Well, that ain't likely, Marv,' said Horan, without turning from the window. 'It's like the judge here says, we leave her for now. Her time will come. As it will for Charlie Toon for his part in all this. Meantime, we stay easy, relaxed, let the town simmer down.'

'Easier said than done, Sheriff,' said Slaney. 'The boys are beginnin' to enjoy themselves. Just listen to them back there.'

'Let them, for tonight,' grunted the judge, wafting aside a fog of smoke. 'Ain't no harm to that. Tomorrow is another day . . .'

Cassie reined her mount to a halt in a swirling cloud of dust and shielded her eyes against the shimmering heat haze and glare of the Panflats.

High skies and space for as far as the eye could see in any direction. She sighed and turned her cheeks to the soft breeze that always blew across these empty lands, glad for this moment at least to be alive and free.

'Feels good, don't it?' said Doc Sims, reining quietly to her side. 'Town, Horan, trials and hangin's seem a million miles away,' He wiped the sweat band of his hat, settled it again and let his gaze sweep across the scene. 'Times when I got things to figure and need the space to think is when I ride out here, just sometimes to ride, feel the emptiness, the freedom. Does you good, gets to solvin' most things.'

Cassie smiled and sighed again. 'Ain't so sure about it solvin' the problems we got, Doc.' She squinted at him. 'You sure this is a good idea?'

Doc narrowed his gaze on the far horizon. 'Ain't nobody I know to been out to the McCrindle place since they cleared the stock and brought the bodies to town. Ain't exactly been a queue for takin' on the spread neither. Who'd want to this soon after the killin'? But I've just got this feelin' gnawin' in my old bones that the place ain't had its full say. There's somethin' out there nobody's seen yet or been lookin' for.'

'Like what?' said Cassie.

Sims shrugged. 'That I don't know. Mebbe nothin'. Mebbe I'm chasin' round my own shadow, or just gettin' plain past it. On the other hand . . .'

Cassie reached between the mounts to pat Doc's arm.

'We'll go see. Can't do any harm.' She swung her gaze back to the ground they had covered since leaving town. 'Nobody botherin' to follow. You figure Horan ain't much fussed where we are or what we're doin'? He ain't tried to stop us or bring me in.'

'Nor will he,' said Sims. 'My bettin' is he's lookin'

for a few days to let things cool off. Sure, he'll raise a posse to go hunt for Quarry, but there'll be about as much heart in that as there is in stone. Fact is, Horan ain't sure which way to jump now he's accused Quarry of the McCrindle killin's. Can't go accusin' some other fella, can he. Town wouldn't wear that. No, I figure we'll be left alone, leastways for now.'

Cassie flicked the reins between her fingers.

'Then we'll ride.' She smiled.

'Just a few miles now to the west,' called the doc above the steady beat of hoofs. 'Can't miss the place.'

Did the ghosts of those so brutally murdered still haunt the place, refusing to leave as if demanding their right to be there? Cassie shivered at the thought in spite of the morning heat, and reined her mount to a slow walk into the shadows of the McCrindle home.

The place already had the look of having been abandoned, left to the Panflats' searing winds and blazing heat. Dust and dirt had gathered on the porch like squatters waiting for the door to open. The windows were dark and lifeless, the outbuildings silent of the stock they had once housed, the corral empty. Life here, it seemed, had ended – and yet not quite.

'Ain't much to be said for the place now,' said Sims, slipping from the saddle before lending a hand to Cassie. 'Time was when you'd have reckoned for the McCrindles makin' a real go of things. They worked hard, round the clock, every day, come rain, come shine.' His gaze saddened. 'Sometimes don't seem to be no real justice, does there.'

'Just what did happen here that night?' murmured Cassie. 'Does it make any sense?'

'That my dear, is the path we have chosen to walk.' Sims guided her to the porch. 'Let's take a look.'

The door scraped open under the doc's grip, the hinges creaking, a wave of musty air clamouring for the freshness. Cassie moved softly, treading as if walking on coals, a pace or so behind Sims as they came deeper into the main living area. Nothing, she thought, had changed from how it had been left that night; the same clutter, utensils thrown aside in the struggles, a chair overturned, a drawer at the large scrubbed table hanging half-open. Fingers had tried to claw there for perhaps a knife in their desperation to stay alive. She caught her breath sharply at the dark, dried stains of blood on the dusty floor.

Sims took her hand. 'You got the stomach for this?' he asked. 'You don't have to—'

'No, no, I'm fine,' said Cassie, tossing her tied hair nervously into her neck.

Sims grunted and led her gently across the room, passing a curtained alcove.

'Alice's space,' he explained – and on to the bedroom, a gloomy, spider-webbed area shrouded in a grey light from the small, tight window shading what remained now of the bed and its vermin shredded mattress. More bloodstains had dried and crusted on the floors and walls.

Cassie shivered and hugged herself. 'What we lookin' for?' she whispered anxiously.

'Whatever it might have been, I think we're too late,' said Doc, stepping to the roughly carved and polished table at the far wall, where the only drawer had very obviously been rifled. 'Somebody's been here before us. Take a look.'

The drawer was small, compact, where a person might have kept something personal, perhaps a memento, a special piece of jewellery, a letter or a document. Now there was no more than some loose trinkets, a length of ribbon, a coin and a still pristine hawk's tail feather. Dust on the table's surface had been hurriedly disturbed.

'This would have been her drawer – Louise's – somewhere special,' said Cassie, turning over the items. 'A woman's only private place in the home.'

'My reckonin' entirely,' said Sims. 'Now just who would want to see into it – it weren't done on the night I was here, you can be sure of that – and maybe take somethin' from it? What were they lookin' for? Did they find it?'

'I'd wager they were here only hours ago,' mused Cassie, lifting the tail feather to the light. She replaced it tenderly and turned to Doc. 'What now?'

Doc rubbed a finger across his chin. 'Back to town,' he concluded quietly. 'I've a notion that whatever's comin' up will be surfacin' right there.'

They had returned to the porch and closed the homestead door behind them, when Cassie's sharp intake of breath lifted Sims's gaze to the glare-drenched bluff on the horizon.

'My God,' he croaked, shielding his eyes to bring the dark, silhouetted shape of the mounted rider into sharper focus. 'So he ain't made a run for it.'

76

CHAPTER TWELVE

Deputy Frank Johnson finished the last mouthful of steak, mopped his plate with a thick chunk of bread, chewed noisily for a moment, and then leaned back in his chair at the corner table in Slaney's bar and contemplated the prospect of a bar girl for a tasty dessert.

He fancied the dark-eyed, raven-haired, Spanish-looking girl they called Anita. She was vibrant, fiery, handsome in a rugged sort of way. A girl of the mountains, like one of the dancers he had once seen south of the border.

The border . . . he reflected, leaning forward again to settle his elbows on the table. Maybe that is where he should be heading right now, shaking off this town once and for all, and, more to the point, shaking off doing Horan's dirty work. Not that he minded the killing side of it as long as the money stayed good.

But when it came to being duped by a woman . . . he fingered the bandage covering his head-wound from the night before . . . when it came to that, he drew a line. You bet.

And in any case this whole business with Quarry was getting out of hand. Who was to say where the fellow had holed up since his escape? Who was to say what he was thinking? That fellow had given nothing away; hardly said a word, showed no feelings, no emotion, nothing. He had just stared through them ice-blue eyes, that nerve in his cheek, like it was a silent tongue, mouthing his thoughts. Just that. A dangerous man who might get to doing most anything, given the provocation.

So maybe Harold Penney had had a point back there on the Pan. Maybe now was the time for pulling out.

Harold, of course, had not figured it through. He should have known he would be watched, that Horan would never let him go just like that. Horan was not planning on anybody leaving town, and living. There was too much at stake, too much that might be said. But there were ways if you knew where to look for them. If you had a Colt and could use it.

The deputy stood up, nodded to the potman busy with his besom on the far side of the bar, and sauntered to the batwings. Maybe he would forget the girl until later, get to his planning instead. No time like the present. Who could say what another day might bring?

He fingered the bandage again, pushed open the batwings and stepped out to the shaded boardwalk.

It was exactly three minutes to two o'clock on that hot afternoon when Frank Johnson turned his slow gaze over the sunbaked street, paused to adjust his hat to the glare and headed for Charlie Toon's livery.

The saloon-bar clock was striking precisely two when the first shot rang out.

It was followed in rapid succession by two further shots, all three hitting the deputy in his chest in an aim that was as calculating as it was deadly. Johnson's arms flew high above his head on the initial impact, his body twisting and turning through the second and third shots, his eyes widening, bulging, mouth lolling open stupidly. He hit the dirt with a thud that raised a cloud of dust and hovered on the sunlight like a swarm of glittering flies, and did not move again.

The first sound to break the eerily empty silence was the scream of a bar girl at Slaney's saloon. Then a dog barked, somebody closed a window, another swished open. A customer at Hinton's mercantile rushed from the store to the boardwalk, still clutching a length of fabric. Horses in the livery stables snorted noisily. Charlie Toon stopped work at the forge and stared wide-eyed through a cloud of smoke and steam.

Otis Slaney slopped a measure of whiskey down his best brocade waistcoat and cursed. Judge Bream stirred in his sleep but did not wake. The bullock-chested man pushed a girl from his bed and told her to get dressed.

The old-timer, dozing quietly in the rocker on his back porch, opened his eyes, pondered for a moment, and decided that the noise he had heard had indeed been gunshots. Only then did he stand upright as best his old bones would permit and wander towards the main street.

It took Sheriff Horan two minutes to buckle his gunbelt, don his hat and rush from his office to be the first to reach the body.

'What happened here? Anybody see anythin'?' Sheriff Horan frowned into the sea of faces peering at the body. 'Well?' he snapped, coming upright from his squatting position. 'Did you or didn't you? Fella don't just get shot in broad daylight and nobody see anythin'.'

'This one did!' quipped the old-timer, blinking furiously as he smacked his lips.

'I did, I saw somethin',' said a youth at the back of the throng.

'What? What did you see?' growled Horan, easing a passage for the youth.

'Up there, on the roof, other side of the street. There was a man up there. Saw him. Sure I did.'

'Who was it?' called somebody deep in the crowd. 'Did you see him clear?'

'I'll do the questionin' here if you don't mind,' said Horan, noting from the corner of his eye that Judge Bream and Otis Slaney had joined the bar girls on the saloon boardwalk.

'Doc's on his way,' shouted another man.

Horan cleared the passage again and ushered Doc Sims to the body. 'Ain't nothin' to be done,' he murmured. 'Shot clean through.' He swung away to face the youth. 'So what did you see, son? Spit it out.'

'Yeah, let's be hearin',' urged the bullock-chested

man. The youth stuck his thumbs in the belt at his waist.

'Weren't that clear, o'course. Couldn't be, not with the light behind him like it was. But he were there, sure enough.'

'F'cris'sake, boy, *who* was there?' steamed Horan.

'That man,' blurted the youth. 'The one who did for the McCrindles. The one we had standin' to trial. John Quarry.'

The silence was instant, then thickened until it seemed no one dared to speak.

It was Judge Bream from the shaded boardwalk who eventually broke it.

'You sure about this, boy, absolutely sure?'

The youth began to sweat, shuffled his feet in the dirt.

'Sure I'm sure,' he said, his eyes flicking nervously over the watching faces. 'Weren't no doubt. I saw plenty of the fella back there at the trial, and it was him on the roof. It was John Quarry who shot Frank Johnson, so help me God.'

'He never left. The sonofabitch stayed right here. Crept into town like a rat and took out Frank.' Horan paced the length of the saloon, smashed a clenched fist on a table, turned and paced back again to face Judge Bream, Marv Hinton, Otis Slaney and, in the deeper shadows at the back of the bar, Doc Sims. 'So where is he now? How'd he get into town like that in the first place?' He seethed between clenched teeth. 'That Cassie's got a lot to answer to, and when I get my hands on her—'

81

'Too late to go wastin' your time on that,' said the judge, opening a new bottle of whiskey. He poured a measure, sank it and helped himself to another. 'You've got only one thing, and one man, to concentrate on. The whereabouts of John Quarry.'

'What's he plannin' on?' said Hinton, squinting across the deserted bar to the still-sunlit street.

'Retribution,' clipped Slaney, selecting a cigar from a box on the bar. 'Some sort of punishment for the treatment we meted out here.'

'Like shootin' folk,' said Hinton.

Horan turned his gaze on Doc Sims. 'You got anythin' to say on this, Doc? Your so-called client tell you what he had a mind for? Or mebbe Cassie knows.'

'Cassie don't know any more than I do, which is nothin',' returned the doc. 'As to what's happened here today – all I ask is, why Johnson? What made Quarry select your deputy, Sheriff? Any notion?'

Judge Bream paused midway through a gulp. Hinton's mouth opened and closed, suddenly parched and dry. Slaney blew a twisting cloud of smoke and peered through it with tight, narrowed eyes.

'What you sayin' there, Doc?' murmured the saloon-keeper. 'I hope you ain't suggestin'—'

The batwings swung open under a flurry of arms and legs.

'He's been seen again,' gasped a lean, pale-faced man tumbling into the bar. 'John Quarry. Up at the livery. Large as life. Turned all the horses loose, every last one. There ain't a mount in town!'

82

CHAPTER THIRTEEN

Charlie Toon told his story to a suddenly crowded, jostling livery where every square foot of the space, every bale of straw, box, crate and barrel had been occupied by the town men, their gazes concentrated, their silence as fragile as glass.

'Just crept in, must have,' said Charlie, conscious of Judge Bream and the sheriff flanking him like turnkeys. 'Never saw him, never heard nothin' 'til he stepped close, comin' out of the shadows, and had a barrel in my back.'

'What did he say, Charlie?' asked a man perched on a pile of straw bales.

'Let him tell the story,' glared Horan. Charlie wiped a lathering of cold sweat from his face.

'Didn't say a deal,' he went on. 'Words don't seem to rate much with him. Just said as how I was to do exactly as he said, no questions, no messin'.' He swallowed and nodded his thanks to Doc Sims for the offer of a hip-flask of brandy. 'Tied my hands with that rope there, gagged me, then set about freeing up the horses and leadin' 'em real quiet to the back.

Seemed like he had a feel for the animals. Know what I mean?'

'I seen fellas like that,' slapped the old-timer, sucking on an empty corncob pipe. 'Kinda put a spell on the beasts so's they go soft as kits to whatever's said. Weird it is. Fella out Oregon way—'

'All right,' snapped Marv Hinton, 'let Charlie do the talkin' here.'

The old-timer grumbled behind the pipe. Sheriff Horan sighed. Judge Bream looked on enviously as Charlie took a deeper swig from the brandy flask before handing it back to Doc Sims.

'All happened real quick after that. Fella didn't say no more. Just cleared the stables 'til there weren't the sight of a horse. Only the smell of 'em . . .' Charlie swallowed again, stared blankly for a moment, then continued: 'Guess they'll all be grazin' the Pan by now. Goin' to take some roundin' up.'

'Never mind that,' urged Horan irritably. 'Where did the fella go? Did you see where he went?'

'Not a thing,' said Charlie. 'Fact is, I didn't even know he'd gone. He just disappeared. Faded away like some mist or somethin'. I was strugglin' with the rope bindin' me when Pete there arrived and raised the alarm.'

'So he's been gone some while now,' said Slaney, brushing the back of his hand across his moustache.

'All of an hour, I'd guess,' offered Charlie.

'And that leaves us with precisely nothin', goin' nowhere,' pondered the judge. 'We don't know where the fella is. We don't know why he's really here, and now he don't intend us havin' enough mounts to team up a handful of supply wagons, let alone raise a decent posse.'

'Some of them Pan homesteaders have got horses to spare,' called a man at the stable doors. 'Mebbe they'd help.'

'And how far do you think you'd get to ask 'em?' grimaced Horan. 'Quarry would stop you inside a quarter mile in any direction. Same as he'll control exactly who's comin' in.'

'You sayin' as how we're as good as tied down?' said the bullock-chested man, thrusting his hands into his pockets.

'Seems that way,' croaked Hinton.

'But that ain't right,' piped a voice from the throng. 'Hell, how can you be a prisoner in your own home? 'T'ain't natural.'

'But that's the way of it,' said Slaney. 'Might as well face up to it 'til we've got the sonofabitch under lock and key again.'

Horan stepped up to stand astride a crate. 'And that's precisely what we're goin' to do: put the sono-fabitch back where he belongs – behind bars.'

' 'Til we get to the hangin',' quipped a man in the shadows.

'You're right,' grinned Horan. ' 'Til we get to the hangin'.'

'And how we goin' to catch the rat?' sneered bullock-chest. 'Don't tell me we're goin' to ask him round to Slaney's for a drink!'

The town men laughed and joked among themselves. The old-timer sucked noisily on the corncob. Otis Slaney stifled a wry grin. Marv Hinton and the judge squirmed in their coats. Doc Sims watched the throng of faces carefully as tension gave way to welcome relief.

'Not quite,' boomed Horan above the babble. 'John Quarry is nobody's fool, that we can be certain of. He's smart, knows his way about – but come the end of the day, he's human. He's goin' to get hungry out there on the Pan. He's goin' to need fresh water, but above all, he's goin' to have to bring to a close whatever it is he's here for. Sooner or later he's goin' to make his move. So we wait for him to do just that. We wait – but we don't relax a muscle. We watch, stay sharp, seal this town tight against every nook and cranny. There ain't goin' to be nowhere John Quarry can hide or pass through without we know to it. When his shadow moves, we want to see it. When he breathes, we want to hear it.'

Horan stepped clear of the crate. 'That's what we're goin' to do, beginnin' right now. John Quarry will be behind bars again in a matter of hours.'

'But he won't, will he?' said Cassie, clearing the plates from the supper table in Doc Sims's front parlour. 'Horan's runnin' scared of the fella. He won't get to Quarry, not nohow.' She bustled away to the kitchen. 'Not, at any rate, if I know John Quarry.' She came back to the parlour, a cloth in her hands, a frown darkening her face. 'But do I know him? Mebbe not. Damn it, I barely said two words to him. Question is—'

'Question is, what was Quarry doin' out there on the Pan this mornin'?' Sims left the table, crossed to the stone fireplace where logs and kindling lay unlit in the grate and assumed his habitual stance with his back to it. 'Ask yourself how it was he knew that was McCrindle's place when, accordin' to him, he was a stranger to the territory, just driftin' through. Who had told him where the spread was? I hadn't. Its location wasn't raised at the trial. But, if he did know, then he had gone there lookin' for somethin' specific and, by my reckonin', found it.'

Cassie eased herself slowly into a chair at the table. 'And if that's the case, he's still here for only one reason: retribution. He's mebbe figured – or might even know – who was involved in the killin' that night.'

'Penney's already dead, almost certainly murdered by Frank Johnson. Now Johnson's dead. So who's next?'

'We ain't goin' to do no better than guess, are we. But mebbe we should get to talkin' to Quarry, fix a meetin' or somethin'. That's the only way we're ever goin' to find out precisely why he's here.' Cassie stood up. 'He'd talk to us, Doc, I'm darned sure he would.'

Sims was about to reply when a sudden burst of shouting from the direction of Slaney's bar brought him quickly to the door.

'Hell!' he cursed, conscious of Cassie at his side as they stared, stunned and silent, at the licking, swirling flames reaching across the night sky at the rear of Slaney's saloon.

'Where is it? How'd it start?' wheezed Sims as he

joined the snaking lines of town men running towards the blaze.

'Them old shacks back of Slaney's private room,' huffed a man at his side. 'Been fallin' apart for years. Empty, I'm told, but that ain't the point, is it.'

'Don't need to ask who did the torchin', eh, Doc?' wheezed the old-timer, catching up as best he could. 'Guess you've figured that for yourself.' He winked. 'That fella Quarry, ain't it. Sure to be. Just lettin' us know he's about.'

Teams of men who had been drinking in the bar were already hard at work in a chain passing pails of water from bar to fire as fast as they could be handled. Judge Bream stood alone, silhouetted like some grotesque statue in the flickering shadows. Otis Slaney simply stared, a cigar lodged between his fingers, his eyes following the activity as if in a stupefied daze. Sheriff Horan had taken charge the minute the call of 'Fire!' had gone up, his voice bellowing through the darkness and above the crackling, spitting, exploding blaze like a riverboat's foghorn.

'Anybody injured?' gasped Doc Sims, his eyes smarting on the swirls of smoke as he stumbled to join Horan.

'Not to my countin' so far,' croaked the sheriff, directing a new team of men into line. 'Pretty well got it under control. Be over in another hour. Thank the Lord there's no wind. Small mercy.' He growled and spat. 'This is Quarry's doin'. He's here, and it don't look like he's leavin'.' He spat again. 'Well, we'll see about that come noon tomorrow.'

'And what's that supposed to mean?' said the doc, wiping the beading sweat from his brow, his eyes narrowing against the heat and glare.

'I got my own way of dealin' with things, Doc. Been figurin' for some time that what this town needs is a bit more weight, a tighter grip. So now I've done somethin' about it.'

'Done what, f'cris'sake?' frowned Sims, his voice lifting above the crash of flaming timbers.

'Sent a message south a few weeks back before all this started. Got a long-standin' friend works out of them Mexican towns.'

'What sort of friend?' persisted Sims, blinking the smoke-sting from his eyes.

Horan turned his dirt-streaked face to the doc and stared at him in silence for a moment.

'A friend who knows how to handle himself, who's been around some, if you get my meanin'.' He grinned. 'Not to put too fine a point on it, Doc – a gunslinger, name of Paget. You'll see.'

CHAPTER FOURTEEN

Cassie hesitated before crossing the few yards of street-dirt to the boardwalk, the glowing lights, noise and buzz of conversation beyond the batwings to Slaney's saloon bar.

She sniffed, catching the smell of smoke, embers of fire, things old that had finally gone up in flames. She lifted her gaze to stare at the still thick and shrouded night sky where even the brightness of the moon had been temporarily obliterated, and took a deep breath. The fire had been doused, the saloon's outbuildings reduced to little more than ash and charred timbers, but no one had died – only a half-dozen or so had suffered the effects of smoke and heat – and the town was still standing, its familiar colourless self.

But for how long, she wondered, before the news Doc Sims had brought her became a reality and the gunslinger, Louis Paget, hit town? She shivered in spite of the night's balmy air, straightened the fit of her shirt, and stepped briskly to the boardwalk, paused at the batwings, took another deep breath, and joined the crowded bar.

The silence descended as if dropped like a deadweight from a great height. Men stared, but said nothing. A bar girl prised herself from the grip of a hairy-chested man and pushed through the throng to Cassie's side. Another kicked herself free of a lap and joined her. Cassie calmed them both and held their hands in hers.

'Got a nerve showin' your face here, ain't you, gal?' growled the bullock-chested man, easing from the bar. 'Hope you ain't come to apologize for what you did. Bit late now. Frank Johnson's dead, we've spent the best part of the night tamin' that blaze back there – and all thanks to you, Cassie. Freein' up that fella Quarry was a bad choice on your part. Time you were behind bars, in my opinion. What do you say, boys? Shall we pen her?'

The bar girls pressed themselves closer to Cassie.

'Handlin' her's goin' to be a whole heap of fun,' sniggered a flushed-faced youth.

'You'll keep your hands off her – all of you,' called Slaney from the open door to his private quarters, a Colt lazing like a half-asleep cat in one hand of his folded arms. 'You lookin' for me, my dear?' He grinned. 'I hope so for your sake. 'T'ain't exactly healthy round here.' He stepped to one side and gestured to the open door. 'Shall we?'

Cassie detached herself from the bar girls, smiled reassuringly at them and threaded her way carefully through the throng of men.

'See you later, gal,' quipped a man, landing a hand on her butt.

Cassie passed into the shadowy, lantern-lit gloom of Slaney's private room without a word.

Marv Hinton sat with his back to the wall, his eyes empty, staring into space, hands flat on his knees, shoulders slumped. He looked up quickly as the door closed behind Cassie and Slaney, but said nothing.

Judge Bream was seated at the baize-topped table, a bottle of whiskey and a glass within reach. He too looked up, grunted and poured himself a generous measure.

Slaney placed the Colt on the table, took a cigar from his pocket, lit it and blew a thin line of smoke to the ceiling.

'Good job for you I was around,' he murmured, eyeing Cassie carefully. 'Could have got ugly out there.'

Cassie tossed her hair and stiffened her shoulders.

'They wouldn't have lynched me if that's what's botherin' you. That would have been a waste. They'd have had other plans for me.'

The judge grunted. Slaney grinned and blew more smoke. The storekeeper's fingers clawed at his knees.

'But I ain't here to discuss the rabble out there,' continued Cassie, 'or John Quarry and whatever trouble he's givin' you – plenty by the look on your faces. I'm here to ask just what in the name of whatever sanity you've got left – any of you – in gettin' yourselves tied in with a scumbag type like Louis

Paget.' She paused to gaze over the faces suddenly turned towards her. 'Horan has told you about callin' in a gunslinger, I take it? He's certainly told Doc Sims.'

The judge finished another measure in a single gulp.

'We know all about Paget,' he said, hooking his thumbs into his waistcoat as he leaned back. 'We've always known, since we'll be payin' for him to be here.'

'So what's the thinkin'?' said Cassie, fixing the judge's stare with her own. 'Don't tell me you're offerin' a home and a decent livin' to the ratbag, because believe me, Paget works only one way in any situation, any place. And that comes at the end of a gun.'

'You know Paget?' asked Slaney.

'We've crossed. A long time back now, but I ain't forgotten, and I'm tellin' you, all of you, that Louis Paget is like callin' in the very dregs of hell itself.' Cassie paused, watched the concentrated faces gleam as if coated in steam. 'Paget works strictly for money, straight cash,' she went on. 'You name your target, he does the rest. No questions asked. And if it's protection you're lookin' for, you'll get it with Paget. He just shoots, kills, maims anythin' that threatens. He takes what he fancies when the fancy hits him – and that means everythin'. This town ain't much right now, but it don't deserve Paget. I'm warnin' you, if he sets foot in this town—'

'Horan's choice of assistant in maintaining law and order in Faithfull, is entirely his decision,' growled the judge, leaning forward again. 'But he has the

93

backing of the town's foremost citizens, be assured of that.' His wet eyes opened wide. 'And that is final.'

Cassie stiffened again. 'Only reason for a rat like Paget darkenin' this town is because somebody's scared of somethin'. Or mebbe you see Paget as an answer to Quarry.'

'I'd watch your tongue there,' croaked Hinton. 'You've done more than your share of damage round here.'

'Speakin' of which,' Slaney grinned, his back to the door as he locked it, removed the key and slipped it into his pocket, 'I figure you owe me some, Cassie. All that cosyin' up to Doc Sims has kept you from your job.'

'You can forget that,' flared Cassie, a flush rising in her cheeks, her head beginning to pound. 'I'm puttin' Faithfull behind me just as soon as . . . And you can unlock that door. I've had my say. I'll leave you to Paget. You've been warned, but mebbe you deserve him.' She took a step forward. 'Now stand aside there.'

'Not so fast,' said Slaney, moving to collect the Colt from the table. 'We ain't through yet, are we.'

'Where is she?' said Doc Sims, elbowing his way through the crowd to the bar. 'Where's Cassie?'

'Back there in Slaney's room,' bullock-chest nodded, with an uneasy glance at the door to the proprietor's quarters. 'Been there best part of an hour.' He shrugged. 'Her own doin', Doc. She should've stayed out of it. Got some nerve comin' here in the first place.'

'Wouldn't be in her boots right now,' piped a fellow shuffling cards at a table. 'Did enough trouble at the jail – and look where that's leadin' us. No sayin' what another day's goin' to bring if we don't get off our butts and rope that Quarry fella in fast. I'm for that – a posse. Get him, dead or alive.'

'That's for me.'

'Me too.'

'Dozen of us could ride out from here and have him in hours.'

'After we've spent a couple of days tryin' to round up enough horses to do the job, that is. Can't be done.'

The crowd murmured its agreement.

'And even if you had the horses you'd be ridin' round out there like dogs chasin' fleas,' said Sims, his voice cutting icily across the bar. 'You don't think Quarry's goin' to be out there conveniently waitin' on your showin' up, do you? You don't figure for one minute—'

'All we figure for doin', Doc, is bringin' him to book for the killin's at the McCrindle spread,' snapped a man standing at the end of the bar. 'And stayin' alive ourselves before Quarry gets to pickin' us all off one by one, or torchin' the whole darned town.'

' 'T'ain't John Quarry you should be lookin' to . . .' began Sims, only to fall chillingly silent as the door to Slaney's back room was opened and Cassie was bundled like something half-dead into the bar, blood trickling from her mouth, her eyes glazed into a dazed stare, her shirt torn and hanging limp from bruised flesh.

'Anybody wants to help himself to what's left, is welcome,' sneered Slaney from behind a cloud of cigar smoke.

Sims pushed his way to catch Cassie in his arms as she fell forward.

'You'll pay for this, Slaney,' he croaked. 'Mark my words, you'll pay.'

The rifle shot that followed blazed from somewhere in the night beyond the batwings, shattering the glass and mirrors behind the bar to a shower of flying fragments and splinters.

CHAPTER FIFTEEN

Sheriff Horan stared across the bar at the shattered strips and fragments of mirror facing him, the hanging pieces of glass distorting and exaggerating his features so that he suddenly had only one eye, half a mouth and nothing at all where his left cheek should have been.

He grunted quietly to himself and turned slowly to focus his gaze on the faces of Slaney, Judge Bream and Marv Hinton, and beyond them to the silent, staring town men still filling the smoke-hazed saloon.

'Quarry,' he said, the gaze fixed now on Slaney. 'Quarry fired the shot that did this.' He spat purposefully and deliberately into a spittoon to his right. 'Mebbe it weren't such a good idea to go treatin' Cassie the way you did. Mebbe you made a mistake there, eh? Not very smart.'

'Got what was comin' to her,' said Slaney, fingering strands of his moustache. 'Hell, she teams up with Doc in that crazy notion of defendin' Quarry – walks out on me, *me*, the one who gave her a roof and money and kept her in them fancy-frilled dresses.

Not content with that, she then goes and sets that scumbag killer free.' He thrust back his shoulders and swung his fiery gaze to the devastation behind the bar. 'And now, this. All her doin'. Oh, yes, she got what was comin', and there's mebbe more yet.'

'Where is she now?' asked Horan.

'Left with Doc,' said Hinton. 'She'll be back at his place.'

'Never mind her,' piped a man in the crowd. 'What about Quarry? Where's he right now?'

'Any place,' called another. 'But you can bet he ain't far. Somewhere in town.'

'Just waitin' on pickin' off his next target,' added a third man to the general murmuring and agreement of the throng.

'All right,' said Horan, raising his arms for quiet. 'I hear you, every last man, and you're right, Quarry is here. There ain't no disputin' that, and mebbe he is close, but that ain't no good reason for us gettin' our boots wrong-footed. We ain't goin' to get to the rat by scurryin' about with our pants on fire.'

'You got a better way?' called the bullock-chested man.

'As it happens, yes, I have,' said Horan, watching closely as he drew the men's attention.

Judge Bream opened his mouth to speak, thought better of it and looked round for a handy bottle and glass. Marv Hinton dusted unseen specks from his coat. Slaney fumbled for a cigar and lit it.

'We've got help comin',' announced Horan. 'Real help. Professional. A man hired for his special talents, the sort of talents we need to get Quarry either behind bars again, or dead.'

'A gunslinger,' clipped the old-timer.

'Call him what you will, it don't matter none.'

'A gunslinger,' repeated the old man. 'There's only one word for the likes of hired killers.'

The sheriff dismissed the man with a cutting glance and concentrated again on the crowd of town men. 'A fella by the name of Paget – Louis Paget – will be here by noon tomorrow. He'll be workin' alongside me and the judge here. You will all co-operate with him in helpin' to lay our hands on John Quarry, the killer, I might remind you, of not only the McCrindle family, but probably Harold Penney, and my deputy, Frank Johnson.' He paused a moment before adding, 'And now you can all go find your homes. Right now. Bar's closed. We've got a busy day comin' up.'

Doc Sims eased the collar of his coat into his neck against the dawn chill and watched the first smudge of light slip across the eastern skies. He shrugged his shoulders, thrust his hands into his pockets and walked slowly to the end of the veranda at the rear of his home.

Quiet enough now, he reflected; sleeping town, most folk either dozing or dreaming, even Cassie had succumbed at last to her exhaustion and slid into a deep sleep in the doc's spare room. She had taken some cruel treatment at Slaney's hands, but Cassie was no loser and a whole sight tougher than most men. She had had to be to survive a past where there had been any amount of the likes of Otis Slaney. And worse –

the likes of Louis Paget.

She had recounted what she knew of the man with a cold glaze to her stare.

'Hit this part of the world from somewhere back East, and came with a reputation. A dozen dead men, and mebbe more, behind him; any number of beatings, but he generally favours a kill. He don't like leavin' nobody still standin' once the unfortunate fella is in his gun sights. Does his job, takes his money and whatever else he fancies, and rides on to the next hell. Seems now like it's our turn under Horan's biddin'. Well, I just hope he knows what he's buyin', 'cus there ain't nobody here who could hold a candle to the likes of Louis Paget. . . .'

But where, wondered Sims, turning to pace back again, did that leave John Quarry?

He had already proved himself more than capable of ensuring his own survival and fighting back against an injustice that had come within a spit of seeing a noose round his neck. But he had not put Faithfull behind him. He had not ridden hell-for-leather for the refuge of the mountains. He had chosen to stay. And to visit the deserted McCrindle spread.

Revisit the spread might be a truer description, thought Sims, pausing to watch the light gather strength. Quarry had known exactly where to find the home, and had entered it knowing precisely what he was looking for. Maybe he had found it. Maybe he had found what he had been heading into Faithfull for in the first place.

Sims fumbled in his coat for a cheroot, lit it and blew the smoke deliberately into the lift of the slow morning breeze. Supposing, he mused, that the man had started out . . .

He went no deeper into his thoughts as his gaze suddenly narrowed and focused on the silhouetted shape of the mounted rider on a distant bluff. How long had he been there, wondered Sims, the cheroot idling a wisp of smoke in his fingers? Quarry, was it him? The shape seemed familiar. Was the man watching or waiting?

Sims blinked and half-turned at the appearance of Cassie at the open doorway.

'I woke kinda sudden,' she murmured sleepily. 'Thought I saw somebody, or heard somethin'. Mebbe I was dreamin'.'

'No,' said Sims, taking her hand. 'No, you weren't. In fact . . .' He swung round again to the shifting light and open land beyond the veranda. But now the bluff was empty, the rider gone. 'Well, mebbe you were, my dear, mebbe you were.'

The town men gathered early in the street, some with the sleep still in their eyes, some with a look of uncertainty close to fear in the shiftiness of their glances, others taking a bolder, more determined view, their curiosity now getting the better of them as they sought the shady boardwalks to await the arrival of Louis Paget.

' 'Bout time we got tough around here,' swaggered a lanky youth, his hat slouched to an angle. 'Been too soft for too long. Quarry ain't goin' to know what's hit him when Paget gets here.'

'Gunslingers don't never do good,' grunted an

old-timer. 'I seen plenty. That time back at Bootstrap when a fella name of Will Green shot his way clear across the territory. He didn't do no good. Died like they all do, eatin' dirt to a faster gun.'

'I ain't fussed none who Paget is or what he's done,' said a man seating himself astride a barrel. 'If he brings that Quarry fella to book, that'll be fine by me. Same goes for most other folk.'

'Gunslingers leave stains,' murmured the old-timer. 'Always have. Always will. You'll see.'

'And not long now,' said bullock-chest, consulting his timepiece. 'Anybody seen anythin' of Doc or Cassie this mornin'?'

'Cassie's still at Doc's place,' offered a man in the deep shade, 'but I seen Doc headin' for the livery a while back.'

'Mebbe he's for ridin', if he's still got a horse,' sneered the lanky youth. 'Take the woman with him while he's at it. She ain't long for this world if she hangs about here much longer.'

'Never mind the woman,' said the man on the barrel, 'what about them horses we suddenly ain't got? We're goin' to need horses, damn it, and soon.'

'Well, mebbe your gunslinger will take care of that too!' quipped the old-timer.

The men continued to lounge and smoke, spit, talk endlessly and debate among themselves, their gazes rarely straying from the haze of the dusty trail that reached into Faithfull from the south.

It was exactly noon when they fell silent at the sound of an approaching rider.

CHAPTER SIXTEEN

His shadow lay thick and brooding in the dirt like something about to strike, a darkness that seemed to swamp and be the substance of the man and his mount where they waited at the head of the street. Dark horse, dark-eyed rider, dark hat, dark clothes; only the lighter shade of the bone butts to his twin Colts catching the sun's glare.

He sat the horse under a tight rein as his gaze ate into the town and what he could see of it: the dusty street and its lines to left and right of familiar buildings; doors, windows, boardwalks, hitching-rails, scattered curls of smoke. Nothing moving save the busy flies and one man's jaw as it worked a wad of chewing baccy. He took in the watching faces, his stare lingering over each one as if sampling it; flicked like a blink of light when the man astride the barrel shifted his position, moved on again until he had consumed every inch of all that lay within his view. Then he loosed the reins and walked the mount on to the scuff of slow steps.

The bullock-chested fellow swallowed deeply and

eased his hands slowly to his pockets. The old-timer narrowed his eyes and grunted knowingly: 'I seen 'em all before.' A man stepped carefully for a better view, fearful that the movement might disturb or not meet with approval. Another cleared the sweat from his face and was suddenly chilled in the nape of his neck. The lanky youth straightened his hat. 'Ain't he just somethin' . . .' he murmured vacantly.

Horse and rider came on until they reached Sheriff Horan's office where the man reined up, dismounted, hitched the mount and strode purposefully to the already open door and thudded it fiercely shut behind him.

Only then did the men in the street come out of what had seemed like a trance.

Marv Hinton had opened his store at the usual time, but there had been few customers save those whom he rated his regulars and others, like old Ses, who came through his doors simply to chat.

' 'T'ain't goin' well,' he had begun, seated on the stool at the counter from where he had a clear view through the open doors to the boardwalk. 'You can smell it ain't.'

'How come?' Marv had asked with only a polite interest as he continued to replenish a back shelf.

'One of them there human things, ain't it. Sweat and fear and that. Comes out of the pores. Oozes so's you can smell it. You smell it?'

'Can't say I do,' said Marv, sniffing instinctively on the familiar store smells.

'You will, you will, specially now there's a

gunslinger about. Yessir, ain't nothin' like a
gunslinger for raisin' a smell.' The old man sniffed
loudly. ' 'T'ain't that fella Quarry they need to worry
about so much as the gunslinger. Oh, I seen 'em
before. Did I ever tell you about that time back at
Murgatroyd when that young goofer name of
Smithson took on—'

'You did, you did, many times,' halted Marv,
wiping his hands through the apron at his waist. 'And
I ain't for hearin' it again, not today anyhow. Why
don't you go take yourself off to Slaney's for a while,
get to hear first hand what the town's sayin'.'

'Can tell you that without goin' to Slaney's to hear
it. Town's moanin' about Quarry and him bein' on
the loose, and losin' all them horses from Charlie
Toon's like they have, that fire back of Slaney's and
what really happened to the barber. And now whatever we've got comin' up with that gunslinger. And
I'll tell you somethin' else they'll be talkin' about . . .'
Ses tapped a finger on the side of his nose. 'They'll
be sayin' as how there's a whole sight more to this
than meets the eye. Oh, yessirree, they'll be sayin'
that all right.'

'And what's that supposed to mean?' said Marv,
forgetting the shelf to lean across the counter
intently.

'It means, Mr Hinton, as how not everybody hereabouts is goin' along with what they say happened
out there at the McCrindle spread. Mebbe it didn't
happen like it's been assumed. Mebbe Doc Sims has
a point about John Quarry and producin' some
evidence to say as how it was him out there that

night. And another thing . . .'

The old man leaned closer. 'I ain't got it for gospel yet, but there's been a whisper about to say as how Quarry's been seen at the McCrindle home. That's right – *seen*, large as life. Now why would he be doin' a fool thing like that when he could ride and be clear of the territory faster than blinkin'? Why would he want to go back? What was he lookin' for? Would you have a notion as to that, Mr Hinton?'

The old man's gossip had raised many notions in Marv Hinton's thoughts, all of them enough, he reckoned, to close the store for lunch and go in search of another's opinion, hear what he had to say about the outlook.

'I ain't fussed a deal right now.' Slaney had smiled, pouring two full measures of whiskey in his coolly shaded private back-room, ' 'specially now Paget's ridden in. You met him yet?'

'No, I haven't,' said the storekeeper irritably, anxious to move to other matters. 'I'm more concerned about what's bein' said around town. Ses tells me—'

'If you believed every word Ses puts about, you'd think this town was some fast-livin', high-falutin city back East!' Slaney placed a glass in Hinton's hand. 'Drink up. We ain't got nothin' to fear so long as Judge Bream's with us and Paget stays sharp. He's bein' paid enough.'

'But what about this talk of Quarry bein' seen out at the McCrindle spread?' persisted Hinton. 'And what's he doin' here, anyhow? I tell you, if we don't do somethin'—'

'You ain't thinkin' of doin' what Harold got into his head, are you? You ain't plannin' on leavin' town?'

Hinton stared into his drink. 'Harold was a fool,' he murmured. 'Shouldn't have done what he did. Askin' for trouble – and got it.' He drank quickly. 'But that don't alter the fact—'

'Make one false move now, and Paget will kill you soon as look at you. He's under Horan's orders. He knows the score about that night. Knows who's involved and what they did. You don't need remindin', do you, Marv? Don't want me to go into all that again. Of course not.' Slaney finished his drink and poured himself another. 'Let's leave Quarry to Paget. I'm sure he'll take care of things.'

Hinton sighed and stepped away to the window where the drapes were only part-drawn against the glare of sunlight.

'Easy enough to say,' he said quietly, 'but things don't never work just as you fancy they might. Nothin's gone as it should since that fella Quarry drew into town. Beginnin' to look to me as how Horan was a whole sight too hasty in jailin' him. Mebbe we should have waited awhile.'

There was a tap at the door, a moment's pause before it opened and the pot-man looked nervously round it.

'Thought you should know, boss, as how Paget's in the bar and askin' for you.'

Slaney smiled and turned to the storekeeper.

'Let's go meet the gentleman, shall we?'

*

The saloon was strangely silent for the time of day and the occasion of an important new arrival. Two groups of town men were gathered in the deeper-shaded areas. A handful watched from the boardwalk, their heads bobbing and passing at the bat-wings like puppets. Others lurked at windows, or stood in shade and what they saw as safer ground on the opposite side of the street. Only three or four had actually got as far as ordering up drinks, and no one had given the clutch of girls so much as a second glance.

Sheriff Horan and Paget stood viewing the shattered glass behind the bar.

'. . . and that's just another good reason for gettin' this fella back behind bars, or wherever. Stop him before he starts any more fires or gets to loosin' another round of lead,' Horan concluded as he lifted a measure to his lips.

Paget merely grunted and glanced without turning his head at the approach of Slaney and Marv Hinton.

'Welcome to Faithfull, Mr Paget,' beamed Slaney, offering a hand which Paget left hovering. 'Just like to say right now that I'd rate it a real privilege if you'd regard Slaney's bar – and its facilities – at your disposal for the duration of your stay.' He smiled broadly, but to no more than another sidelong glance and throaty grunt.

'Same goes for my mercantile right across the street there, Mr Paget,' gestured Hinton, catching the sneering looks of some town men. 'Got a fine selection of most things back there, includin' some fresh in from the East. Mebbe you'd care—'

'Yeah, yeah, I'm sure Mr Paget is grateful,' waved Horan, finishing his drink with a flourish, 'But we've got other matters gettin' the priority right now.' He swung round to face the bar and the newly crowded batwings. 'As of sundown tonight, I'm imposin' a curfew on this town. Nobody ventures out of doors 'til sun-up. Anybody found breaking the curfew will have me to answer to.'

'And Paget,' muttered a town man under his breath.

'You fellas here pass the news around, and if it's a drink you're lookin' to, then you'd best get it now, 'cus it's goin' to be a long, dry night.'

The men murmured among themselves. The bar girls clucked and giggled. Marv Hinton straightened his frock-coat and picked at imaginery dust specks.

Slaney stiffened. 'Goin' to hit business,' he grumbled.

'Let's hope it hits a whole sight more,' said Horan. 'Let's hope it flushes Quarry into doin' somethin' stupid. We'll be waitin' – and that includes you, Otis, and you, Marv. You're hereby sworn in as deputies. You'll be workin' along of Mr Paget here, so make sure you do as you're told.'

Paget continued to stare into the shattered glass, his reflected image shimmering like creeping flesh.

CHAPTER SEVENTEEN

'Never figured it possible to listen to silence.' Cassie watched anxiously from the open door at Doc Sims's home as night settled, but saw nothing in the deserted street save darker shadows and the first faint flickerings of lantern lights. 'Eerie,' she concluded as Sims came to her side.

'Seen anythin' of Horan and his new deputies?' he asked, narrowing his gaze on the unlit saloon and the brighter light at the sheriff's office.

'Nothin' yet,' murmured Cassie. 'Knowin' Otis and Marv, they ain't goin' to take exactly willingly to the job. Not their style. Paget, on the other hand . . . No sayin' to him or where he might be. The night suits him.'

'He'll be out there, you bet. But where's Quarry, that's the real question? And what's his next move?'

'Mebbe he'll pull out now that Paget's arrived. Ain't no point in gettin' himself shot up by some two-bits gunslinger when he could be long gone to the hills. Don't make no sense to walk into trouble, or go lookin' for it. You reckon?'

Doc Sims sighed. 'I'd say that would be the case nine times out of ten, but with this fella I just don't know. There's somethin' – somethin' very deep and personal keepin' him here, and it ain't about just bein' sore over the arrest and that farce of a trial.' His gaze narrowed again. 'John Quarry ain't here by accident, and he ain't stayin' for a love of the place neither. A man who gets clear of a waitin' noose runs for his life. He don't wait on to examine the rope.'

A sudden blaze of light from the sheriff's office spread like a stain across the boardwalk as Slaney and Hinton emerged cradling Winchesters and set off to impose the curfew.

'They mean business,' said Cassie.

'But for how long?' pondered Sims.

It was in his bones now, creeping out of the night like something in search of him. And it was closing.

Marv Hinton tightened his sweaty grip on the cradled rifle and halted to take stock of what he could see. Not a deal. Shapes, some familiar, some that seemed to have bred on the backs of others, some that simply lay there and might have been anything. No folk about, leastways none he could see or sense. Most had taken Horan at his word and stayed indoors.

He moved on. Town was awful quiet, he thought, taking care to walk where he knew from daily use that the boardwalks never creaked. The silence was thick and clinging like black treacle trickling from a pot.

111

Drowning the night. Drowning him.

He ran a finger round his collar. This was going to be the longest two hours of his life. Two hours, he grimaced, before he reported back to Horan and the sheriff took his turn on patrol.

Slaney, of course, would be happy enough. He relished intrigue and action, enjoyed living on the edge. It was his nature – that and making money. Bleak night tonight at the saloon, though. A few days of that prospect and Slaney might just get to protesting. Not that it would do a mite of good. Horan and Judge Bream were never . . .

What was that? A noise. Something shuffling. A footfall perhaps, or had it been a dog sloping off to the shadows? Hard to say. He swallowed, flexed his neck and shoulders against the sting of sweat. Hell, he thought, this was . . . There it was again. The same slow, shuffling movement.

'Slaney?' he hissed. 'That you out there?'

No reply, no movement. The silence again, thick and heavy. Keep moving, he reckoned. Just keep to the boardwalk, places where the planking was safe. And hold to the dark. Never make yourself a target. Hell, he had heard Horan say it a dozen times: *Watch the light. Know where you are. That's how you stay alive . . .*

Marv Hinton halted, noting the glare of a light from a clapboard home at the far end of a narrow alley to his left. Maybe he should get that light trimmed, he thought. Lights at an undraped window could be dangerous at a time like this. Folk should be warned.

But that was as far as the storekeeper's reckoning went on that night. He had half-turned to the light in the alley when he froze where he stood, gasped, groaned and stared wildly into the blaze that seemed now to grow and engulf him as the steel blade at his neck went deeper and the breath in his body shortened and finally expired.

The storekeeper was dead and unmoving in seconds, but the thud as he hit the boardwalk had alerted Otis Slaney where he patrolled on the opposite side of the street.

His hissed call to his partner and the searching probe of his gaze had yielded nothing until he saw the dark mound of the body and, once closer, the steadily thickening pool of blood at its head.

Sheriff Horan came to his full height, from a squatting position, stared quickly into Slaney's ashen face, then grunted and drew Doc Sims aside from the body. He glanced up and down the still deserted night-filled street.

'Quarry,' was all he said.

'I'd reckon,' murmured Sims. 'Another target.'

'What's that supposed to mean? You ain't helpin' if all you can do is go round hintin' and suggestin'—'

'Don't take no hintin' or suggestin' to figure that them who've died these past hours were all out at the McCrindle spread – and so were you and Slaney there.' Sims's stare was steady and fixed. 'Question you've got to keep askin' is: does Quarry intend that you're all goin' to pay for that night? What does he know that he ain't so far owned to? You can't hold a town under curfew for ever. And you can't lock this town up indefinitely.'

Horan's gaze moved back to the body and then, impatiently, to Slaney.

'Let's get this body off the street before the town gets to stirrin'.'

'I ain't much for that sort of thing,' mumbled Slaney, crooking his rifle under his arm as he fumbled in his pocket for a cigar.

'Just do it,' snapped the sheriff. 'Smokin' can wait. Meantime . . .' He peered anxiously into the darkness. 'Yes,' he grinned, 'meantime we'll get to doin' some of our own dealin' for once.' He nodded to the pool of light spilling again from the open door to his office where Paget lounged against the jamb behind a curl of smoke from a glowing cheroot.

'You finished?' called Horan across the night.

The gunslinger raised an arm in acknowledgement and disappeared deeper into the office.

'Now you'll see,' murmured Horan, glancing quickly at the doc. 'Time we played our own hand, show this Quarry fella just who's runnin' this town.'

Sims stiffened, narrowed his gaze, leaned forward and felt a cold chill squirm at his neck before settling in his spine. Paget had reappeared at the open door pushing Cassie, her hands bound behind her, into the pool of light.

'What the hell—' began the doc.

'She's taken hostage,' said Horan, staring across the night. 'If Quarry doesn't give himself up, she dies – any way Paget there chooses to kill her. That's the deal. No compromise.' He turned to face Sims. 'And

114

I'm givin' Quarry 'til sundown tomorrow to make his decision, so I suggest you go look for the fella, Doc, and make him see sense before it's too late.'

It had seemed too late even as Doc Sims had seethed and ranted against Horan's actions but eventually he had to turn from the pool of light at the office, the sneering figure of Paget and the grey fear and despair in Cassie's face, and set about the only thing he could do – find John Quarry.

But where to begin? Damn it, the fellow had been as elusive as a shadow so far – glimpsed only once out at the McCrindle spread – and there was no good reason for supposing he was going to show himself now.

Or had he seen Cassie in Paget's hands and deduced quickly enough what Horan was planning?

The man had maybe lingered even after the killing of Hinton, and now he had the silence and the darkness of Horan's curfew to move around at will.

Sims's first call had been at his clapboard home to assess whatever damage had been done by Paget in taking Cassie. Very little, he concluded. There had been no struggle, no fight. Paget had seized his moment; probably been waiting his chance and moved the minute Horan had summoned the doc to Hinton's body. Hell, he thought, he should have seen this coming, should have known that Horan's anxiety would deepen through every hour Quarry remained free.

Now he was playing his strongest card. Maybe the

only card left to him.

Sims's second call, for no good reason that he could rightly explain save for starting his search somewhere, was at Charlie Toon's livery, where he had told bluntly of Hinton's death and the taking hostage of Cassie.

'I've just got to find Quarry,' Sims concluded, accepting the mug of freshly made coffee from the pot on Charlie Toon's simmering forge. 'Time's runnin' out, and I don't reckon for Horan debatin' the issue.'

'Unless Paget gets impatient,' said Charlie. 'Types like him ain't for sittin' about for too long. He'll want to get to usin' them fancy guns, so he might go lookin' for Quarry himself.'

'Or wait for Quarry to come to him with Cassie as the bait.' Doc sighed, sipped at his coffee and stared beyond the forge to the clutter of buildings, shacks and sheds that spread from the line of the main street. 'Where would he be holed up now?' he murmured. 'Where would you be, Charlie, if you were him? Still in town, or would you have ridden out? Plenty of places to hide out there.'

'Well, mebbe,' mused Charlie. 'But if Quarry's doin' what I think he's doin', I'd stay close. Sure I would.'

'And what do you reckon the fella's doin'?' asked Doc Sims.

Charlie thought for a moment. 'I don't know who the man is, but I tell you this, Doc: John Quarry knows well enough what happened that night. He knows that Horan, Marv Hinton, Slaney, Harold

116

Penney and Frank Johnson were liquored up and out at the McCrindle place for only one thing. And they took it – at any price. They killed Herb McCrindle, his wife and daughter.' He stared at Doc through the drift of steam from the coffee-pot. 'I know, 'cus I was there myself, too damned late to stop it. But I saw, sure enough. Oh, yes, I saw it all.'

CHAPTER EIGHTEEN

It was some time before Doc Sims was able to break his unblinking stare into Charlie's face and manage to croak:

'You saw?' and then: 'How?' and more hurriedly: 'What happened?'

Charlie had swilled the dregs of his coffee to a pile of forge ash, replaced his mug on the bench nearby and run a hand over his face as if clearing it of cobwebs.

'Glad to get talkin' about it at last,' he began, 'though, don't you fret, I'd have spoken up at that trial if it had gotten any worse for Quarry. But as for that night . . . Well, I'd been out deliverin' a couple of mares to the Donnell spread, north end of the Pan; stayed on for supper and was a mite late headin' back to town. Gettin' to full dark when I saw the lights at McCrindle's place and heard all the noise – shoutin', then some screamin', a moanin', then shots, mebbe two.

'I figured for the family bein' hit by drifters or the like, and to be honest was feared through at what I might find when I got closer. Then I saw the hitched horses, five of 'em. Hell, that would be some bunch to tangle with, so I figured for gettin' help fast as I could. Came as close as I dared, saw Mrs McCrindle fightin' off some fella; saw Herb's body, and his gal stripped near naked, then, damnit, my horse spooked, a fella came crashin' out of the cabin and all but saw me. But not quite, though I'd seen him. It was Horan. No mistake. And there was no sign of anybody remotely resemblin' John Quarry.'

'So you pulled away?' said Sims.

'Had no real choice, not if I was goin' to see some justice done later. Herb and his gal were dead, Mrs McCrindle as good as, and I knew sure as fate Horan would shoot me to save his own skin. So, yes, I pulled away, and lived with the nightmare ever since.'

Charlie looked round the deserted stabling. 'Now we've reached this. A bad time for this town, Doc, and it'll only get worse if we don't do somethin' about them scumbags out there, help Cassie and find Quarry.' Charlie ran a hand over his face again. 'I ain't the spit of a notion what's really at the back of John Quarry's mind, no more I reckon than you do, but I'm all for findin' out. And fast.' His gaze tightened. 'Let's do this together, Doc. I'll go in search of Quarry. You look to Cassie and keep an eye on that rat, Paget. You armed?'

'Not yet.'

'I've got a spare Colt out the back there. Take that.' Charlie narrowed his gaze on the empty street. 'There'll be a touch of light in a couple of hours and the town'll be stirrin'. We'll meet up again at your place.'

Doc collected the Colt, belted it awkwardly at his waist and slid away again to the night, his mind reeling, his thoughts confused, but his resolve firm enough as he headed for the lights at the sheriff's office.

Cassie shivered and snuggled instinctively into the closeness of her shirt. She rolled her shoulders, pulled at the shirt collar, and stared through the bars of the cell to the drifting cloud of cigar smoke and the two men seated either side of the sheriff's desk, a half-empty bottle of whiskey and two glasses between them.

Otis Slaney had been silent for a full five minutes, his gaze lost to the shadows, his body limp, the carefully waxed moustache dishevelled and stained. He tapped a finger lightly on the desk as if to the tempo of his thoughts.

'Quarry knows, don't he?' he said at last, lifting his gaze to Horan's face. 'He had to know. It's the only explanation.'

Horan poured two measures from the bottle.

'Mebbe.' He pushed a glass towards Slaney. 'Don't let it worry you. Just leave it to Paget, and once we've got Quarry under lock and key again, Judge Bream will take care of the rest.' He gulped his measure and smacked his lips. 'We'll have a hangin' yet, you'll see.'

Slaney's gaze had retreated again to the shadows. 'Been a friend of Marv's for years,' he reflected. 'Shouldn't have died like that, no way. Goin' to miss him. Whole town'll miss him.' The reverie snapped and his gaze flared. 'What we goin' to do about her?'

120

he snapped, nodding to the cell.

Horan half-turned in his chair and smiled at Cassie.

'You hear that, ma'am? Otis here wants to know what we're goin' to do about you.'

'Suit yourself,' huffed Cassie with a flick of her hair.

'Oh, you can rest assured to that, my dear!' grinned Horan. 'You bet we'll suit ourselves, or least-ways my friend Mr Paget will.'

'I ain't much for jokin' at a time like this,' said Slaney, coming to his feet with a scrape of the chair. 'There's Harv's blood out there, damn it. We've lost Harold, Frank Johnson . . . Livery's been cleared of horses, my outback place gone up in flames . . . Quarry's still loose, and now we've got Paget stalkin' the town like some depraved hound. I don't like that fella.'

'Not much of an outlook, is it, Otis,' quipped Cassie, coming to the bars of the cell. 'Fact is, Faithfull ain't a healthy place to be right now. I'd watch my step if I were you.'

Horan stood up, poured another measure for himself and glared at Cassie.

'Don't get lippy. This ain't the place and you ain't got the time.' He glanced at the clock on the wall. 'Be first light in an hour or so. Goin' to be a busy day – specially for you, gal.'

'Well, I ain't waitin' for light,' said Slaney, settling his hat and tugging at his coat. 'I've got a business to run. Lost enough as it is.'

'Sorry I can't oblige with my services,' Cassie

grinned, 'but like you can see I'm a mite tied up at the moment!'

'Cut it.' Horan glowered. Then, turning to Slaney, he growled: 'Paget'll be here shortly, and you're relievin' him on curfew patrol.'

'Damn your curfew!' snapped Slaney, slamming the door behind him as he stomped out to the still moonlit night.

'Fool,' mouthed Horan, finishing his drink.

Judge Bream roused himself from the sweat-soaked bed, heaved his legs to the floor and tried to bring his vision into some semblance of focus.

Tough going. The walls were moving again like slow waves threatening to engulf him. The door seemed unusually small. Two chairs now, close together, one almost within the other, and the floor was lifting and tilting. He might slide off the end of it, tumble into a dark oblivion beyond the window . . . .

He blinked once, twice, three times. Easier now. The window was brighter, the moon pressed against it like a staring eye. He reached for the bottle and glass on the table at his side, poured a measure, drank it in a single gulp, shook his head and focused again.

The room now was gentler, friendlier, still very quiet. No sounds from the rooms to left and right. No clients for the girls. Saloon was closed, the curfew in operation.

He came unsteadily to his feet, took the few paces to the window and squinted into the street below him. All quiet. Nothing moving. A light at Horan's office, another at a home nearby. They had cleared the body of Marv Hinton from the boardwalk. Bad business, he thought, grunting. Nothing was going quite as it should. Quarry was moving about somewhere. And now there was a gunslinger prowling the street. No saying what might happen next, or when.

He was about to go back to the bottle and the bed, when a shadow in the street slid from one side to the other and faded into the darkness of the boardwalk.

He heard the creak of the batwings, the shuffle of a footfall. Slaney returning, he wondered? Had to be. He would help himself to another measure, then dress and go take a look. Maybe Slaney had some news. Time they had a talk, anyhow. There was planning to be done, arrangements to make.

He blinked again, swallowed, and was surprised to discover the walls were not moving and the floor was level.

CHAPTER NINETEEN

Doc Sims had moved from shadow to shadow like something being hunted, conscious at every turn, every step taken, that Horan's newly acquired side-kick might be waiting, looking for an opportunity to flourish his fancy Colts.

He had stood for some time in the deepest shadows to watch Slaney emerge from Horan's office, pause for a moment on the boardwalk as if to gather himself, then stride purposefully across the street to the saloon.

There had been the merest suspicion of another movement – perhaps Charlie Toon, Paget, a town man risking the curfew, even Quarry – but Sims could not be certain and had settled his concentration on the soft light in the sheriff's office.

Did he simply walk in, brandishing his gun, order Horan to release Cassie? Would it be that easy? But where to then? Maybe they could hole up at his home, or the livery. But wherever, Paget would soon be on the prowl.

Did he wait another hour for first light? Maybe this

was not a job for one man. Maybe he could recruit some sympathetic town folk. Strength in numbers. But how many would be prepared to risk the guns of Paget? Could he ask them to take such a risk?

He moved on, still edging closer to Horan's office, still debating how to set about getting Cassie out of the jail. He was within a few steps of coming into the glow of light at the office window, when the sudden creak of the batwings and the thudding of stumbling steps from deep in the saloon to the boardwalk forced him back into the shadows.

He watched bewildered as Judge Bream fell into the street in a flurry of waving arms, flapping shirttails and tottering steps, his eyes as wild and white as moons.

'Horan!' he bellowed at the top of his voice. 'Horan! Get yourself here, f'cris'sake. It's Slaney. Somebody's strung him up!'

The sheriff's door burst open in a sudden flooding of the lantern glow across the boardwalk followed by Horan, a Winchester already gleaming in his hand, his gaze flashing to left and right, then narrowing on the judge, who had slithered to a swaying, lathered halt in the middle of the street.

Doc Sims watched carefully, silently, realizing now that if Horan left the office his way would be clear to reach Cassie. He swallowed, laid a hand on the butt of his Colt, began to sweat in the nape of his neck.

'Where's Paget?' shouted the sheriff.

'I ain't seen nothin' of Paget,' growled the judge, 'and I ain't givin' two spits for Paget right now. I'm a whole sight more concerned about that sonofabitch, Quarry. This is his doin'. Get yourself here.'

'Get some lights lit,' rapped Horan. 'Curfew's over for tonight. And somebody go find Doc Sims.'

Sims swallowed again as he watched Horan hesitate for a moment, glance back to the office, then hurry away to the saloon where the first lights were flickering and shimmering and a handful of bar girls had gathered, sleepy-eyed and hugging themselves into night clothes, at the batwings.

Sims moved quickly. Half a dozen steps and he was into the office.

'Drawer on the left,' hissed Cassie at the sight of him.

He opened the drawer, found the keys and strode to the cell.

'What the hell's goin' on?' Cassie frowned as Sims fumbled the key to the lock. 'Sounds as if Quarry's been busy again.'

'Exactly that,' said Sims, swinging the cell door open. 'Let's go. Horan will be lookin' for me. Get yourself into the shadows for a while. When the coast's clear head for my place, and when Charlie Toon shows up listen real close to what he's got to say about that night on the Pan.' Sims drew the Colt from its holster. 'Here, take this, and don't hesitate to use it, specially if it's Paget in your sights.'

Sims patted Cassie on the shoulder, smiled and waited until she had faded into the thinning night before turning his back on Horan's office and heading for the saloon.

The street activity and raised voices had brought

the town to life again. Lights appeared in windows, doors opened, a dog barked. The lanterns in the bar began to flare to full brightness. The bar girls had retreated.

Sims pushed through the bat-wings without breaking his stride.

'That's as far as you go, Doc,' ordered Horan from his place at the shadowed end of the bar. 'We're too late, anyhow. Slaney is dead. Strung up in his own back room there. Our friend Mr Quarry has a sense of the ironic, don't he? We ain't got to hangin' him yet, so he hangs Otis. Appeals to the sense of the bizarre, so to speak.'

Sims had turned slowly, his back to the back room's open door, to face the sheriff and the levelled barrel of his Winchester. 'I ain't armed,' he murmured, 'so you can ease up on that rifle.' He stiffened and narrowed his gaze. 'As for Quarry, I've been talkin' to Charlie Toon.' He paused to study Horan's slowly changing expression, from the cynically arrogant to the suddenly tensed. 'He can prove Quarry wasn't out on the Pan the night of the McCrindle killin'. He can prove it because *he* was. And he'll swear to it on oath.'

Horan stared as if watching the slow, slithering glide of a sidewinder.

'What else has that two-bit blacksmith been sayin'? His word ain't worth a spit.'

'You can rest assured you and Judge Bream will be gettin' the chance to hear exactly what Charlie's got to say – if Quarry don't get to you first. Meantime—'

Doc had half-turned back to Slaney's room when the tap of the gun barrel on the bar halted him.

'Be very careful what you're sayin', Doc,' said Horan. 'There's enough trouble in this town at the moment without you addin' to it.'

'And let me tell you somethin', Sheriff,' snapped Doc, taking a step forward as he faced Horan again. 'I've heard exactly what Charlie's got to say. I've heard him and I've listened, and if it's of any interest to you and the judge, I'm beginnin' to form my own opinions as to what really happened that night.

'But while I'm here and you've got that Winchester levelled at my gut – and no doubt my back – you'd best get to reckonin' on arrestin' me, because I've just released Cassie from the cells. And if you take my advice, you'll abandon any thoughts of continuing this crazy curfew and get to lookin' to your skin.'

Sims turned against Horan's stunned silence and headed for Slaney's back room. 'And now in the interests of town hygiene,' he said over his shoulder, 'I've got another dead body to dispose of.'

Slaney's bulging, toad-eyed stare was penetrating even though the man was dead, noosed at the end of the rope slung across the room's single beam.

He had been taken, hands tied behind his back, made to stand on a chair to the left of the green-baize table, the noose placed over his head, and only then come face to face with his hangman before the chair had been kicked away.

He would have choked his last within minutes, thought Sims, gazing into the man's staring eyes. He

128

would have writhed, squirmed, fought uselessly against the throttling, choking grip of the noose until there had been no more than a last moaning gasp, and then the creak of rope strained across timber as the body hung limp and lifeless, turning in the momentum of its own deadweight.

Sims cut the rope and lowered Slaney to a heap on the floor. He squatted and peered closer, amused for a bizarre moment to see that the once carefully waxed moustaches had collapsed to strips of over-grown scrub, and chilled in the next to wonder what madness had flared in the bulging eyes on that night at the McCrindle spread.

He sighed and had started to come fully upright when he noticed the folded sheet of paper stuffed roughly into the top pocket of Slaney's rumpled coat. He removed it, stood up and crossed to the dull light of the table lantern and held the sheet to the glow. A scrawled note with the words arranged carefully in a neat, level hand: *This man was one of the five responsible for the killing of my brother-n-law, Herb McCrindle, the raping and killing of his wife, and my, sister, Louise, and their daughter, Alice.* It was signed: *John Quarry.*

CHAPTER TWENTY

'His sister?' Cassie frowned. 'Hell, that would answer a whole heap of questions.' She crossed to the window in the doc's parlour and thudded the clenched fist of one hand to the palm of the other. 'But if that's the case and Quarry knows what happened, then he's known all along, from the minute he rode into town.' She swung round to face Sims and Charlie Toon. 'He knew when Horan jailed him. Knew when Judge Bream conducted that two-bit farce of a trial. Knew when we stood to his defence, and when I set him free. And that's why he's stayed.'

'He killed Johnson, Marv Hinton, now Otis Slaney,' pondered Charlie. 'So who killed Harold Penney?'

'Almost certainly the man who trailed his body in from the Pan – Frank Johnson,' said Sims.

'That leaves only Horan of the five who rode out to the McCrindle home,' mused Cassie.

'And the judge,' added Charlie. 'He might not have been with the others on the night, but he sure as Sunday knew who was and what happened. He's been standin' to them as good as if he'd been involved.'

'A total abuse of his judicial oath – as good as spit-tin' in the face of the law,' said Sims.

'But what next?' asked Cassie. 'What will Horan do? Don't forget he's got that gunslingin' rat Paget to back him. What will Quarry do? Where is he?' She turned to the window again. 'He left the note for you to find, Doc. So what do we do now?'

Sheriff Horan ran a finger along the gleaming barrels of the Winchesters waiting erect and ready in the gun cabinet. He reached the last one, let the finger pause a moment then ran it back to the start.

'Take your pick.' He grinned, conscious of Judge Bream's wet eyes watching him and the lurking presence of Paget at the shadowed end of the office. 'Take 'em all if you have a mind,' he added. 'And assumin', o' course, you know how to use them – accurately.'

'Just what precisely are you plannin'?' wheezed the judge, his breath laced with a mix of cigar smoke and whiskey fumes.

The sheriff selected the rifles one by one from the cabinet and laid them gently across his desk.

'Simple,' he said, without looking at the judge. 'We're goin' to hole up at Charlie Toon's livery. Take it over, just the three of us, you, me and Paget there. And we're goin' to stay 'til the townfolk hereabouts get it into their thick heads that we ain't for foolin' with. We'll demand horses, saddled and ready to ride, and free passage out of town to the Pan. If we don't get them, we'll torch the livery. And that'll be just the start.'

'And Quarry?' croaked the judge. 'What about him?'

'Quarry can go to hell!'

'That he most certainly will not do.' The judge ran a hand over his face. 'You realize what he's done? You do understand, don't you? He very obviously knows what happened that night, and those involved. This is his revenge. This is why he's here, why he rode into town like he did. Damn it, it don't take a lot of fathomin', does it.'

'Who is he?' frowned Horan. 'And how could he have found out? We ain't been shoutin' about it, f'cris'sake.'

'We ain't, but others mebbe have. An episode like that don't go unnoticed exactly, and news of that sort travels fast, even out here. Some traveller passin' through . . . words dropped here and there . . . Pan folk talkin' to drifters . . . a whole heap of possibilities. But I'll tell you somethin'. Tell both of you.' The judge glanced quickly at Paget to draw his full attention. 'That fella Quarry ain't nothin' like what you took him for. He definitely ain't no drifter, never has been, and ain't likely to become one. But as to who he *really* is—'

'Ain't the time for debatin' it, Judge,' drawled Paget, peering closer through the window. 'Looks like the town men are gettin' restive down there at the saloon. Unless you want me to go and put a mark among 'em, I suggest we move.'

'We move,' snapped Horan, searching out the ammunition for the rifles.

*

The bullock-chested man stood astride the board-walk fronting Slaney's saloon, a holstered Colt at his generous waist, a rifle in his right hand, and faced the approach along the dusty street of Doc Sims, Charlie Toon and Cassie. The men surrounding him made no sounds or movements as the trio drew closer.

'We're takin' over, Doc,' called the man once Sims came within earshot. 'Seems to us that Horan's runnin' out of options. We ain't for no more talk of curfews, and we ain't for bein' sweat-scared over Paget. God knows what's goin' on in this town, but whatever it is it's time we got to hear of it, and the feelin' is, Doc, that you know a whole lot more than you've been lettin' on.'

'That's true,' said Sims, coming to the foot of the steps to the boardwalk, 'and you've a right to be told. I'll tell you, but not before you tell me where Horan, the judge and Paget are holed up right now.'

'Still in the office there,' said a youth at the man's side. 'But we don't figure for 'em stayin'. They can't ride out, that's for sure. We're keepin' watch.'

'And Quarry?' asked Charlie.

'Nothin',' said the man. 'But he sure as night keeps himself busy! Is that what this is all about, Doc? Quarry selects his targets like he's got a list.'

'Let's get inside,' said Sims, mounting the steps.

The old-timer put out a hand to guide Cassie. 'Good to see you're still in one piece, ma'am,' he smiled. 'If anybody deserves to survive all this to the

133

end, it sure is yourself.'

Cassie nodded and moved to the batwings.

'I hope the girls have been well treated. Now that Slaney's no longer with us, I think we'll get to ringin' in some changes.'

'Not too many!' quipped a man.

The town men turned at the call of a fellow hurrying across the street.

'Horan's made his move', he gasped, reaching the boardwalk. 'Holed himself up at the livery with Judge Bream and that gunslinger. Says he wants to see you, Doc. You've got one hour.'

'Time enough for me to tell you fellas what I know, what I've learned from Quarry himself, what Charlie Toon saw that night, and what I've figured for myself,' said Sims. 'Come on, somebody go pour some drinks.'

Judge Bream took a measured swig from his hip flask, shook it to reckon the measures still left, and replaced the stopper with a defiant twist.

'Goin' to have to make it last,' observed Horan, scuffing a boot through the loose straw on the stabling floor. 'Just figure for where we'll be in a few days' time: some neat, clean town miles beyond the Pan – Greyrock, or mebbe Bitter Springs, some place like that where there's a decent saloon and any amount of pretty girls. How about that, eh, Judge? That take your fancy?'

'You can keep the girls,' muttered the judge, fumbling to light a half-smoked cigar. He waited until the tip glowed red, then added: 'Should never have got this far in the first place.' He grunted to himself, stood up and wandered to the full morning glare at the open stable doors. He gazed down the gentle slope to the tight gathering of the town buildings. 'Shame,' he murmured. 'Faithfull ain't such a bad place. I could've seen out my years here.'

'Yeah, well, that's as mebbe,' said Horan impatiently. 'Fact is you ain't goin' to do no such thing. You're goin' to help me and Paget get clear of the damned town, and especially that Quarry fella. Suit me just fine if we can see him eatin' dirt before we leave. So let's cut the sentimentality and get to doin' what's necessary.'

'All because of a mite too much liquor and a good lookin' woman you reckoned for takin' at will,' mused the judge, his gaze still flat on the deserted street, the glinting sunlight where it stared into glass windows, the long shadows as black as paint. 'Five of you, all of the same, obsessive mind . . . And I was darn fool crazy enough to use the law to keep you clear of what you'd done.'

Horan crossed quickly to stand at the judge's back, the barrel of his drawn Colt pressed into his spine.

'And you did it willingly enough in return for a free and easy livin'. Right? You bet it's right, and don't you forget it, Judge. We're goin' to need each other right to the end. Partners, eh?' Horan holstered the Colt and laid an arm across the judge's shoulders. 'Have yourself another swig from that flask. I'm sure Mr Paget here will be able to find a means of replenishing it without too much trouble. What do you reckon, Mr Paget?'

Paget eased himself clear of the livery forge and spat noisily into the ash and dirt at his feet.

'We got company arrivin',' he drawled. 'Doc, that livery owner and a couple of others headin' this way.'

CHAPTER
TWENTY-ONE

Cassie shepherded the bar girls to the quieter, shadowed end of the crowded saloon bar and gestured
for their full attention.

'You heard what Doc had to say,' she began, 'and
what he's told you is the truth. The whole truth as we
know it so far.'

'Is Mr Quarry goin' to kill them all – Sheriff
Horan, Judge Bream and that gunslinger they've
hired?' asked a freckle-faced redhead, pulling a
shawl across her bare shoulders.

'Is there goin' to be a shoot-out up there at the
livery?' murmured a girl with long yellow hair.

'What about Doc?' A darker girl frowned, glancing
anxiously towards the batwings. 'Ain't he in danger,
Cassie? Aren't we all?'

A sterner-faced, taller girl with flashing green eyes
tossed her hair into her neck and stiffened.

'One thing's for certain,' she said defiantly, 'I ain't
goin' to miss Otis Slaney one mite. If he was a party

to what happened out there at the McCrindle spread, hangin' was too good for the rat.'

'Well, that's as maybe,' interrupted Cassie with a calming gesture. 'Let's get to lookin' at things as they are. I have no idea what Quarry's goin' to do next, though I can wager a fair guess. And that goes for Paget too. Horan will set him to doin' the killin', but that ain't goin' to concern you, leastways not if I can help it.'

The girls nodded and murmured their agreement. 'But you mustn't risk yourself, Cassie,' urged the youngest of them. 'You've done enough. If it wasn't for you—'

'Never mind that,' said Cassie. 'What I want you to do now is get yourselves settled upstairs and don't move for nobody – nobody – 'til I've seen which way the wind's blowin' through this town. Ain't no sayin' to it any which way right now, but that ain't goin' to last. Meantime you stay clear of everybody, no matter who he is or what he wants. As for Slaney, ain't nobody goin' to miss him, and that includes me.' She paused a moment. 'Any one of you wants to leave when this is all through and it's safe, can do so. I'll see as you're all paid up fair and square. Now shift – out of sight. See you later.'

The girls headed for the stairs to their rooms, threading their way through the calls and slaps of the town men.

'Hands off, boys,' ordered Cassie. 'This ain't the time. Let's just—'

But her words were lost in the sudden crack and roar of gunshots.

138

*

Paget's fancy Colts were levelled, steady and smoking in his grip as his dark eyes stared at the man he had just shot in both legs. He smiled slowly, spat carefully, holstered the guns and turned his back disdainfully on the scene.

'Let that be a taste of what will come if you don't see sense and get busy,' said Horan with an instinctive probe of his Winchester. 'We ain't foolin' none, as you can see.'

Doc Sims beckoned for Charlie Toon and the second town man to give him a hand.

'You'll pay one day,' grunted the doc as they did their best to ease the wounded man to a position where they could drag him away from the livery.

'We'll see about that,' sneered Horan. 'Meantime you just do like I say: round up some horses, get 'em saddled, then keep your heads down 'til we're clear of town. Otherwise, we torch this place, and anywhere else that takes a fancy, and I turn Paget loose with his guns. You got it? And if you happen to see that fella Quarry you can pass the deal on to him. Now get to it!'

Sims, Charlie and the town man moved slowly, gently down the slope from the livery towards the saloon and the waiting group of folk, their colleague slumped between them, his face lathered with sweat and creased in the agony of his pain.

Cassie and the old-timer were the first to come forward as the group approached.

'Let me help there, Doc,' said Cassie.

'Hot water, towels, bandages,' croaked Sims. 'Fella's got lead buried in both thighs. Goin' to have to dig it out. Clear some tables back of the saloon.' He nodded to the bullock-chested man. 'Get some guards posted. Keep a watch on the livery. Horan wants horses, saddled and ready to ride. Round up what you can, but make it soon. I don't figure Horan's patience for stretchin' far.'

'You goin' along with his demands?' said the man.

'Do we have a choice?' returned Sims, gritting his teeth as they manoeuvred the wounded man towards the batwings. 'Alternatives don't bear thinkin' to.'

'Doc's right,' croaked the old-timer. 'Them sonsofbitches'll stop at nothin'. Did you tell them who Quarry really is?'

'I was tempted,' said Sims, disappearing through the batwings, 'but I figured I might just leave it to Quarry himself – if he gets the chance.'

'Sure,' mused the old-timer to himself. 'If he gets the chance. If he's still here.'

'How long you goin' to give them?' asked Judge Bream, wiping an already wet bandanna over his florid face. 'Longer it goes on the worse it gets.'

Sheriff Horan moved silently through the deep shadows of the livery towards the sunlit glare at the open doors to the street.

'Just long enough,' he said calmly, pausing to glance at the sweating judge before moving on to where Paget waited in the shadows. 'Our friend's gettin' jumpy. He don't like the idea of Quarry still bein' around.'

140

'Me neither,' murmured Paget, his slitted eyes shifting tirelessly over the street and its collection of buildings. 'Mebbe it's time I did somethin' about it.'

Horan waited, staring into the glare.

'Takin' a risk, ain't it? Might be a whole sight easier to let Quarry come to us.'

'Why should he? He ain't in no hurry. He can sit this out for as long as he chooses. And when we ride out, he simply follows – for as long as it takes. He's that sort of a fella.'

Horan stayed silent for a moment, his thoughts bristling, his stare hardening in its concentration,

'Where would you begin?' he asked quietly.

'Leave that to me. You just make sure we get those horses, saddled and ready, and keep that judge sober.'

'You goin' alone?'

'I always go alone.' Paget grinned, danced the tips of his fingers over the butts of his Colts and sauntered casually towards the full glare. 'See you,' he quipped without looking back.

It took the gunslinger only seconds to disappear, as if he had melted in the fierce glare of the sunlight. Within five minutes he was a part of the shadows at the back of the line of buildings running parallel to the saloon. He watched silently, fingering the butts of the guns, his senses alive to the slightest movement, the softest sound.

The talk from the bar was muted; no clink of glasses; laughter and giggles among the bar girls, a yelp as a scavenging dog was sent scurrying for cover. No creak of the batwings. Doc Sims would be busy tending to the

wounded man, Cassie at his side, the town men planning, debating, urging a course of action. But who
among them would have the courage to make a move
towards the livery, wondered Paget, and just how many
were out there rounding up horses?

He shifted, broke his concentration on the boardwalk fronting the saloon, but froze instantly as a
shadow up ahead among the crates, barrels and
boxes at the rear of the store began to move.

A dark, powerful shape stalking like a mountain
leopard. In search of its prey, or with it in sight? Paget
sank lower. He watched. Waited. His fingers settled
like moths on the butts of the Colt. A shift too far,
and they would lift into life in a blink.

The shadow-shape halted, half-turned as if to
move away to the bulk of a worm-eaten shack where
the door hung drunkenly from a single rusted
hinge. Paget's eyes narrowed. A line of sweat beaded
on his top lip. A raised voice in the depths of the
saloon nagged at his concentration. He squatted.
The silence thickened again and the shape moved
on.

Quarry, it had to be Quarry, thought Paget, his
teeth gritting, a flickering grin twisting at his lips.
And unless he was much mistaken the fellow was
unaware of being watched. Probably still reckoning
on Horan sweating it out at the livery. So much for
the man's arrogance, damn him! The grin flickered
again. Fingers danced briefly on waiting butts. The
batwings at the saloon creaked. Hell, somebody
heading into the street? Maybe it was the doc with
another deputation on its way to parley with Horan.

142

No time to find out. He went back to his concentration on the shadow.

But now it had disappeared.

CHAPTER TWENTY-TWO

Paget hesitated, licked his lips, fingered the gun butts absently. The voices and creaks at the saloon had subsided and faded into the eerie silence of a town and its folk in the grip of fear and uncertainty.

He eased softly from one shadow to the next, crouched low behind a broken crate, narrowed and tightened his gaze on the seemingly empty shack and its leaning door. Had Quarry disappeared inside?

Another raised voice from the saloon bar. The scrape of a chair. He shifted again, this time to the cover of a stinking barrel where fat black flies were gathered like a scab on the sticky leftover of the contents. He screwed his nose against the smell, moved to his right and for a split second lost his full view of the open door to the shack.

It was too late when he concentrated again.

The space had been filled by the tall dark shape of Quarry, a Winchester levelled and steady in his grip, his eyes glinting, his expression without the faintest flicker of emotion.

'Spill the guns, Paget,' he said coldly. 'Nice and easy, then step aside.'

Paget's arms had moved as if to be fully raised, but his glare had darkened and the half-grin of cynicism slid to a sneer. He shrugged.

'Don't know who you truly are, fella, but you've had one helluva time hereabouts.' Paget's spread fingers danced on the air. 'One helluva time. Why, I was beginnin' to figure you for—'

The gunslinger's right hand had dropped through the air like a hawk to its prey, settled on the butt of a holstered Colt, drawn it and blazed a line of lead almost before the man had taken a breath. And for a moment in the sudden roar of shots it seemed that Quarry had not moved so much as a muscle, let alone blinked or brought the Winchester into action.

But it was Paget who was lifted from his feet, thrown back into a clutter of crates and boxes and who lay spreadeagled in the store's backdoor trash under the roar of the rifle.

Quarry stepped quietly from the shack to the body, kicked aside the drawn Colt where it had slipped from Paget's grip, and removed the gunslinger's hat. Turning, he skimmed it through the air from the rear of the mercantile to the middle of the street. He smiled softly to himself and tightened his hold on the rifle.

When he left the body where it lay and disappeared back to the shadows, the scab of black flies had deserted the stinking barrel for a more promising feast.

*

'See that?' blustered the judge, gesturing with the hip flask. 'Did you see that, damn you?'

Sheriff Horan stared into the dusty street, his gaze dark in its concentration on the mocking absurdity of Paget's hat stranded in the dirt.

'I see it,' he growled out of the depths of his throat.

'You know what it means? It means Quarry's taken out Paget – just like that. Easy as spittin' grit.' The judge swigged heavily from the flask. 'So what you goin' to do now? What's your plannin' from here? Tell you something, it'd better be good. Damn good. Do you realize—'

'Will you just shut that mouth of yours,' growled Horan, this time turning his glare from the street to the judge's sweating face. 'Talkin' ain't helpin' none right now. You just listen real good to what I'm sayin'.'

'So say it,' snapped the judge. 'Get to it before Quarry gets to us.'

The sheriff moved carefully to the shadows at the side of the open door. His gaze tightened to the left, then the right. He grunted.

'Paget got it wrong, like I knew he would,' he murmured.

'Oh, you did, did you?' quipped the judge. 'You have it right, Paget got it wrong, and he's the professional gun – *was* the professional gun. Well, if you're so smart—'

'He went in search of Quarry, 'stead of lettin' Quarry come to him,' continued Horan, disregarding the judge's sarcasm. 'Fatal,' he added flatly, his gaze shifting left to right again. He waited, grunting quietly to his thoughts. 'Right,' he said at last stepping back to face the judge whose eyes were lost behind the raised hip flask. 'Here's my thinkin' when you're all through with the booze. . . .'

Doc Sims eased aside the growing handful of town men, the inquisitive bar girls pressed around Cassie, and examined the body of Paget with no more than a grunt.

'Best get him out of the heat before he begins to stink,' he pronounced.

'Been doin' that best part of his life!' quipped one of the men to a chorus of only half-committed laughter.

'Hell,' said another, pushing closer to the body, 'does this mean it's over, Doc? Horan and the judge are standin' alone. They ain't goin' to fight on, are they?'

'Let's go take 'em now,' urged a wild-eyed youth. 'Enough of us here to storm that livery. It'd be over in minutes, sure it would.'

'Go easy on my livery there,' countered Charlie Toon. 'That happens to be my home.'

The mood of the men began to change from a chilled fear to a mounting bravado. One of them spat across the body. A taller man slapped a bar girl's butt and called for a round of drinks. Cassie chastized her brood for leaving their rooms and ushered them towards the shadows.

'A toast to Quarry, that's what I say!' piped a man standing at the rear door to the saloon. 'It's him who's seen us through this. Him who's had his revenge – and rightly so by my reckonin'. Now all he's got is Horan, and he ain't no problem. Give it an hour and—'

The man's words were lost on the sudden crack of a rifle shot, followed by another, a third, until the town men stood silent and suddenly ashen at the sight of Sheriff Horan at the open window of one of the saloon's upstairs rooms, a Winchester scanning the gathering like a venomous antenna waiting to strike.

'Get them girls out of sight again,' hissed Doc Sims. 'They shouldn't be here. Should've stayed indoors.'

Cassie made to herd the girls away, but was halted by Horan's rasping shout.

'Hold it right there, Cassie,' he ordered. 'Leave the girls and get yourself up here. Now! No arguin', or I start shootin'.'

Sims cursed under his breath. Cassie shuddered. The bar girls began to sniff and dab at welling tears. The town men stayed silent, their gazes lifted to the window, the glinting barrel of the rifle.

'Where's Quarry?' croaked Charlie Toon.

No one answered, no one moved as they watched Cassie cross slowly to the rear door of the saloon, her whole body tense with the cold of new fear.

'Shift it!' bellowed Horan. 'Meantime, you got them horses ready yet?'

Charlie took a careful step forward. 'We got 'em. Two, saddled up and ready to ride. They're hitched far end of the street.'

'You bring one of 'em – just one – to the front of the saloon,' said Horan, his gaze chillingly indifferent. 'The judge ain't goin' no place, I fancy.'

'He's ridin' out on him,' murmured a man.

'We'll do as you say,' called Sims, 'but there ain't no need to hold Cassie. You've got my word we'll let you ride. Just let her go.'

The rifle barrel ranged menacingly.

'I'll make the decisions on what I do,' snapped Horan. His gaze settled on Cassie again. 'Keep movin',' he ordered. 'Nice and easy.'

'Don't do it, Cassie!' yelled a youth, elbowing his way through the pack of men. 'Stay where you are. We'll—'

The rifle blazed. The youth was flung back like something blown effortlessly on the wind. Sims swallowed and sweated. Charlie Toon gulped. The town men were silent and still. The youth did not move or make another sound.

'I ain't foolin' none here,' growled Horan. 'Now do like I say: get that horse. And you, Cassie, get in here.'

'Do it,' groaned Sims, his eyes wet with grief and hatred.

CHAPTER TWENTY-THREE

The saloon bar was deserted. The shadows long and thick. Shafts of sunlight pierced the windows like accusing fingers. Bottles, some empty, some sampled, used glasses and cigar butts littered the stained tables. Chairs had been pushed hurriedly back to stand as if scattered in panic across the wooden floor where, at the bar, a pool of spilled beer glinted like a monstrous eye.

Cassie waited in the deepest shadows at the rear, her eyes wide, her limbs numb, a cold sweat beading at her brow, trickling down her neck. She shivered in spite of the clamouring heat of the bar and listened for the sounds of Horan, approaching or watching. Nothing. Silence. No movements, save a fly drifting from table to table.

She took a step towards the batwings, her glance flitting quickly to the stairs, the shadowy balcony and doors to rooms. No sounds, no shapes she did not recognize. Maybe she could get clear, she thought, make it to the wings, the boardwalk.

Where the hell was Horan? What had happened to Quarry?

She waited again. Sniffed. The air was heavy with the smells of booze, smoke, men's sweat, cheap scent, fear. She licked her lips, tasted salt, swallowed and caught her breath at the softest tread to a creaking floorboard.

She knew that creak. Had heard it a thousand times. Every day – and night – of her life in Faithfull. Above her. Third door to the right. There was a loose board at the threshold to the room.

Horan was moving.

Her stare settled on the balcony, narrowed to pierce the shadows. She would see him before he reached the stairs. But did she have the time even now to get clear of the bar? Would Horan shoot to kill? He would, she decided. He was desperate enough. A cornered rat with only one way to run from here.

Another creak. Another step. Still nothing of a shape, nothing to see. The town men out back began to murmur. Would they make a bid to storm the bar? Would Doc allow them? Damn it, could he stop them?

She would risk it. Make a dash for the 'wings and trust to whatever luck she still had in credit.

'Stay right where you are, Cassie. Not another step.'

Horan grew in the shafted light at the head of the stairs like something easing from the woodwork. She could see the beaded sweat on his face, the glinting stubble, the piercing glare of the man's eyes. He levelled a Colt, firm and steady.

'Sorry it's come to this, Cassie, but there ain't no other way. You're my guarantee out of here.'

'Where's the judge?'

'Still boozin'. Got a feelin' he ain't goin' to make it. Leastways, not along of me. He's a liability.' Horan took a step down the stairs. 'Let's shift, shall we?'

Cassie swallowed, licked at sweat, ran her hands along her thighs.

'You won't make it,' she croaked from a parched throat. 'It's too late. There's still Quarry.'

'Yeah, there's still him – for now. He don't spook me none.'

'He should.' Cassie swallowed again. 'Louise McCrindle was his sister. He'd somehow heard of what happened out there on the Pan that night. The men, the killing, the rape. He was here to seek his retribution.' She shivered. 'You chose the wrong man for your purpose the mornin' he rode into town. You chose the man who'd returned to find the killers of his sister. You were already puttin' the noose round your neck that day.' She sneered. 'You're a fool, Horan. Just a fool!'

There had been a look of disbelief, shock, and then grim realization on the sheriff's face, but it had lasted only seconds before waning to a sneer, a vicious spit, a glistening of new sweat, a glare.

He came down the stairs in a rush and was already reaching for a hold on Cassie when he halted at the ominous click of a gun hammer, the shift of a boot to boards, the measured tones of a calm, careful voice.

'Tell it how it happened, Horan. Exactly how it happened that night. From the beginning.'

The sound of Quarry's voice fell across the silence as if cutting through it. Horan stayed motionless, his hand still poised to reach for Cassie, his eyes flitting rapidly from left to right, back again; probing, piercing, searching through the shadows for the shape. But there was nothing.

Cassie took a deep breath, shuddered, sweated, wanted suddenly to make the break for the 'wings in spite of Horan's tight, levelled Colt. She shuddered again, relaxed with a toss of her hair and concentrated on Horan.

The sheriff wiped a slow hand across his mouth, and narrowed his gaze.

'Should've noosed you long back, mister,' he croaked. 'Should've done it that first day, 'stead of wastin' time on that trial.' His eyes were still working, still searching, the Colt still levelled. He glanced quickly at Cassie as if to threaten should she so much as shift a limb.

'Did you plan it that night?' came the voice again. 'Did you ride out, all of you, with murder and rape in mind? Had you been figurin' on it for days, mebbe weeks? Plottin', plannin' how you'd do it, where you'd begin, how you'd feel? Was that how it was?'

Nerves were twitching in Horan's cheek, at his temple, in his grip. The Colt lay heavy for a moment.

'You killed them all. Herb, my sister Louise, young Alice, every last life of that family out there on the Pan who'd done you no harm, done nothin' save be

there. Every last one while you took your plea-
sure . . .'

The voice droned on, flat, measured, as if caught
on some ghost wind from the empty plains.

'It was the liquor,' blustered Horan. 'It was the
night, the heat. It happened . . . just happened.'

Cassie shivered. Now she could see her chance.
Horan's concentration was broken. He was somewhere back with the blood, the screams, the nightmare.

She lunged for the nearest table, pulled it between
herself and Horan and turned towards the 'wings.

'Damn your eyes!' cursed the sheriff, loosing a
blaze of lead that was neither steady nor aimed. Glass
shattered, bottles and glasses crashed to the floor.
Horan plunged after Cassie, settled a grip on her
arm and flung her across the bar to the far wall.

'Sonofabitch!' he cursed again and spun round to
face what he reckoned were the shadows hiding
Quarry. He blazed more lead blindly, carelessly, the
fear and panic bubbling in the sweat that lathered his
face, his neck and back, fixing his shirt in a sodden
black plaster.

'You murdered them all, Horan,' echoed the
voice, this time from the other side of the bar. 'Herb
McCrindle, his wife, their daughter. You left nothin'
save the wrecked bodies and the blood. . . .'

Horan spun round, the sweat flying, eyes lit like
flaming coals in a dark grate, levelled the Colt with
his arm stretched to the full, but never got to closing
a finger on the trigger.

Quarry's Winchester roared to set even the shadows shaking. Horan was hurled back, across tables, chairs, through spinning shards of glass, slivers of splintered timber to sprawl dead in the thickening stream of his own blood.

CHAPTER
TWENTY-FOUR

'And it was right here, folks – this very spot – twenty minutes after John Quarry shot Sheriff Horan, that they found Judge Bream hangin' from this beam, the empty hip flask at his feet. He'd taken his own life. Died by the noose he'd been so ready to condemn others to face. Yessir, some kind of justice I guess you'd say.'

Charlie Toon gazed over the faces of his intrigued audience, walked the length of the livery to the open doors and paused in the full glare of the afternoon sun.

'It all happened ten years back,' he mused as the audience followed to his side, 'but it seems like it was just yesterday.' He smiled and turned to the faces watching him. 'You folks are privileged. Stage-route north now stops overnight in Faithfull and you get to seein' first hand the real-life settin' to a part of our history – not to mention meetin' face to face some of the folk involved: Doc Sims, Cassie, proprietor these

156

days of the saloon right there, myself, and still a good few of the original town folk.'

'You're right, Mr Toon,' said a snappily tailored passenger, easing aside the folds of his frockoat, 'it sure is a fascinatin' story. But tell me, what happened to Quarry? Did he just ride out?'

'Just that. Time Cassie had come back to her senses in the saloon, Quarry had gone. Just faded into the shadows. Next thing, Doc and the town men had reached the bar, heard her story and learned of what the judge had done, then somebody shouts to say Quarry's all mounted up and waitin' at the top of the street. We all rushed out, o' course, crowded like flies right there front of the saloon, but all Quarry does is tip his hat to the ladies, smile and wave, then head out due west, crossin' the Pan. Trail would have taken him to within a spit of the McCrindle spread. We figure he mebbe paid his last respects, and left. But to where . . . Well, who knows?'

'And do you think he will ever be back?' asked a middle-aged lady adjusting a pince-nez in her prob-ing stare.

'We'd sure like to think so, ma'am.' Charlie smiled. 'Heck, we still have a heap of questions to have answered, not to say thanks to express. If it hadn't been for Quarry, we'd still be sufferin' Horan, and he'd still be coverin' up for himself and the others for the dreadful things that happened here. As it is, we have a smart new sheriff name of Frank Dennis, a new store-owner, a fresh face at the barber's, and Cassie at the saloon. And we have a future, ma'am, somewhere safe and decent to develop for the young. Damn it, we

got the stage and the likes of you good folk already!
That's somethin'.'

'I still find it all very sad in spite of that, Mr Toon,'
said a well-dressed, yellow-haired young woman
sporting a fashionable Eastern hat. 'That poor family
at the homestead who died so horribly; the note Mr
Quarry left, framed right there in the bar, and the
people – such as yourself, Mr Toon – who must still
be haunted by it all.'

'Oh, yes, ma'am,' said Charlie, 'there's all that
sure enough. You're right, can't deny the sadness,
can't escape the memories. But there's a hard-
workin' young couple pullin' the McCrindle spread
into shape, and there's all this: our town. John
Quarry won it back for us, and we're proud of that,
real proud.' He smiled and gestured in the direction
of the street. 'Shall we walk on, folks? Town's full of
interestin' places, every one of them with a tale to
tell. For instance. . . .'